# Praise for FOR GIRLS ONLY:
## Wise Words, Good Advice

❀

"There are so many dumb advice books out there that it's a pleasure to find one that really works. Carol Weston, advice columnist for *Girls' Life* magazine, does what many parents of adolescents cannot: She resists the urge to drone on. Weston, herself the mother of two daughters, doesn't talk down to her young readers. She doesn't preach. As a result, her advice about school, family, and friends is appealing to an age group that very much wants to know the answers but automatically tunes out parental lectures." —*USA Today*

"Carol Weston is one of the few writers who can quote Cindy Crawford, Goethe, Mother Teresa, Billie Holiday, Francis Bacon, and Tom Cruise in one slim volume and make it work. Weston's unpretentious advice isn't preachy, just chatty—absolutely the right approach for teenagers and parents." —*Columbus Dispatch*

"Carol Weston encourages and guides young minds on everything from smoking ('It's unhealthy, addictive, smelly, and expensive') to love ('Falling in is fun. Stepping in is wise')." —*San Antonio Express-News*

# Praise for FOR TEENS ONLY:
## Quotes, Notes, & Advice You Can Use

❦

"Carol Weston, author of *Girltalk* and the Melanie Martin books, talks directly to teens with advice straight from her heart and mind. Each short essay starts with a quotation. With wise words from notables like Pablo Casals, e. e. cummings, and Wallace Shawn, along with up-to-date advice from such successful female role models as Jennifer Aniston and Alicia Keys, Weston's breezy book offers advice that young adults may actually take to heart. Never didactic, always comforting, Weston writes in a just-chatting-with-you-on-paper style and she knows her audience. . . . A grown-up with valid advice, she's more like a fun aunt or older cousin than a mom or a teacher. . . . Appealing . . . inspiring . . . a treasure trove." —*Bookpage*

"Sage advice . . . inspiring quotes . . . all presented in an understanding and straightforward manner. Weston is known for her previous outstanding self-help books, such as *Girltalk: All the Stuff Your Sister Never Told You*. This book follows suit with a writing style to which teens—both boys and girls—can really relate, almost as if the author is in the room having a conversation with them. Other books use different approaches. . . . However, none use the technique of maneuvering numerous quotes as effectively as Weston does in this title." —*School Library Journal*

"A collection of wise words from just about everyone you can think of, from Aesop to Langston Hughes to Madonna. Solid guidance for teens facing the problems of growing up." —*Atlanta Journal-Constitution*

# For Girls Only

# Other books by CAROL WESTON

For Teens Only:
*Quotes, Notes, & Advice You Can Use*

Girltalk:
*All the Stuff Your Sister Never Told You*

Private and Personal:
*Questions and Answers for Girls Only*

The Diary of Melanie Martin

Melanie Martin Goes Dutch

With Love from Spain, Melanie Martin

From Here to Maternity

How to Honeymoon

Girltalk About Guys

# CAROL WESTON

# For Girls Only

*wise words, good advice*

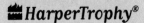 **HarperTrophy®**

*An Imprint of HarperCollinsPublishers*

# For Elizabeth and Emme

Harper Trophy® is a registered trademark of
HarperCollins Publishers Inc.

For Girls Only
*Wise Words, Good Advice*
Copyright © 2004 by Carol Weston

Library of Congress Cataloging-in-Publication Data
Weston, Carol.
   For girls only : wise words, good advice / Carol Weston.
      p.   cm.
   Originally published: New York: Avon Books, 1998.
   Summary: Contains quotations and advice, drawn from a wide
variety of sources, on topics such as friendship, love, and self-esteem.
   ISBN 0-06-058318-5 (pbk.)
   1. Conduct of life—Quotations, maxims, etc. 2. Girls—Conduct
of life. [1. Conduct of life—Quotations, maxims, etc. 2. Quotations.]
I. Title.
PN6084.C556W47  2004                          2003056737
O82'.0835'2—dc22                                     CIP
                                                            AC

Typography by Karin Paprocki
❖
First paperback edition, 1998
Revised Harper Trophy edition, 2004
Visit us on the World Wide Web!
www.harperchildrens.com

# *Acknowledgments*

❀

To Elise Howard for having the best idea ever.

To my husband, Robert Ackerman, and our teen daughters, Emme and Elizabeth. Lizzi read the entire second edition this weekend, pencil in hand, and made helpful comments such as, "Mom, you have enough Euripedes and Goethe! Put in Jennifer Aniston."

To Tui Sutherland, editor extraordinaire, and Gwen Morton.

To fellow collectors of quotations, proverbs, and words of wisdom, including Robert Masello, Mary Biggs, Barbara Rowes, Marlo Thomas, Carolyn Warner, J. M. and M. J. Cohen, Karl Petit, William Cole, Andrew Carroll, Bergen Evans, and John Bartlett.

To Matilde Reategui, Kyla Brennan, Maureen Davison, Laurel Davis, Molly Woodroofe, Hannah Judy, Sue Hipkins, Vanessa Wilcox, Mark Weston, and Marybeth Weston Lobdell (my mom).

To the reviewers and readers who liked the original *For Girls Only*. Hey, I like you right back!

And to the many women and men who spoke so quotably in the first place, and the many excellent journalists who got their words down.

Thank you!

# Contents

✿

Introduction                               1

You You You                                3

Friendship                                31

Love                                      59

Family                                    87

School                                   111

Work                                     135

Parting Words                            159

Your Favorite Quotations                 181

Index                                    191

# Introduction

*The beginning is the most important part of the work.*

*—Plato*

❀

When I was a girl I loved quotation books. I waded through volume after volume looking for lines that spoke to me. What I found were great men's words on war, honor, death. What I wanted was good advice on love, friendship, pimples. And while I dog-eared Ben Franklin, Mark Twain, and Oscar Wilde, I also wanted to hear from women. And Asians. And African Americans.

*For Girls Only* is a book of wisdom and inspiration. I selected hundreds of quotations relevant to girls, then added my own spin. You'll find lines from Aesop and Buddha, Homer and Halle Berry, Queen Elizabeth and Queen Latifah, the Dalai Lama and Jennifer Lopez, Anne Frank and Oprah Winfrey, Sophocles and Sarah Jessica Parker. Not to mention Ben

Franklin, Mark Twain, and Oscar Wilde.

I hope this book can serve as a compass and guide, as well as an introduction to some of the world's most wonderful voices and proverbs. ("A proverb," wrote Miguel de Cervantes, "is a short sentence based on long experience.")

Might boys enjoy this book? Why not? But while *For Teens Only* is for everyone, *For Girls Only* is just for girls—and especially for you. I've been writing for girls ever since, at age nineteen, I wrote for *Seventeen*, then later wrote my first book, *Girltalk*. Who knew that *Girltalk* would stay in print for decades, I'd be the "Dear Carol" advice columnist at *Girls' Life*, and that my husband and I would now have teen daughters of our own?

As you read *For Girls Only*, you may want to flip through, pausing on pages that catch your eye or searching for the quote you need for your essay or letter or yearbook. Or you may want to heed the words of Lewis Carroll, who wrote, "Begin at the beginning, and go on till you come to the end: then stop." (The very last pages are blank—they await your own favorite quotations.)

Is it possible to distill the wisdom of the ages into one slim volume? No. Even the best mix of bons mots would fall short. But it was fun to try. And to quote Steve Martin: "I think I did pretty well considering I started out with nothing but a bunch of blank paper."

❀

# *You You You*

*To love oneself is the beginning of a lifelong romance.*

*—Oscar Wilde*

❀

Love yourself. Love the things that make you you. Your values and talents and memories. Your clothes, your nose, your woes. If you love yourself, you can jump into your life from a springboard of self-confidence. If you love yourself, you can say what you want to say, go where you want to go.

The world can be a tough place, and some of the billions of people out there will try to knock you down. Don't join them. Do things that make you proud, then take pride in what you do. And in who you are.

Who are you anyway? What makes you you? How are you like your siblings and neighbors and friends? How are you different? If you were your own secret admirer, what would you most admire?

"My great mistake, the fault for which I can't forgive myself," Oscar Wilde wrote, "is that one day I ceased my obstinate pursuit of my own individuality." Keep pursuing your individuality. Keep being yourself. Becoming yourself. It can be comforting to dress and act like everyone else. But it is grander to be different, to be unique, to be you.

**I'm the only me in the whole wide world.**

*There is always one true inner voice. Trust it.*

—*Gloria Steinem*

❀

Sometimes it's hard to know who you are and what you want and whom you like and why you like that person. The answers change because you're changing. Growing.

But deep inside, you are you. You were you as a baby, you were you as a kid, and you are you right now.

"Let me listen to me and not to them," wrote Gertrude Stein. It makes sense to consider the advice and opinions of other people. But don't let their noise drown out your inner voice. And don't let the way you sometimes talk or behave in front of others make you lose sight of who you are when you are alone, when you are most you.

"You can live a lifetime and, at the end of it, know more about other people than you know about yourself," aviator Beryl Markham cautioned. Get acquainted with yourself. Tune in to the dreams you have by day and by night. Blend in when you choose to, but appreciate what sets you apart. "The more I like me, the less I want to pretend to be other people," said Jamie Lee Curtis.

**Anybody can be one of the crowd.**

*Being a teenager is a confusing time.*
*That's the lovely thing that happens as you grow older:*
*You are more confident and more loving of yourself.*
*It's easier to say, "You know, that's just not me."*
—*Vanessa Williams*

❀

It takes years to discover who you are and to understand the rules of the game. Years to figure out how to be loyal to yourself and respectful of others. Tom Cruise said, "I truly believe high school is just about the toughest time in anyone's life." The good news: Confidence is cumulative. As Alanis Morissette sings, "You live, you learn."

Adolescents and adults have always had difficulty appreciating each other. Here's what Socrates wrote way back in 400 B.C.: "Young people nowadays love luxury; they have bad manners and contempt for authority. They show disrespect for old people . . . contradict their parents, talk constantly in front of company, gobble their food and tyrannize their teachers."

Some strife is inevitable. But respect between generations is a worthy goal, and harmony gets easier.

**No one ever said it was easy.**

*Self-esteem is a fragile thing.*

—*Gwyneth Paltrow*

❀

Many girls are in a mad rush to grow up. But you can't hurry puberty or confidence. And would you really want to? Why not revel in your one and only chance to be the age you are now?

Besides, everyone feels awkward. Everyone is going through this. "Life is like playing a violin solo in public and learning the instrument as one goes along," wrote Samuel Butler.

Appreciating yourself and becoming introspective does not happen overnight. "I loaf and invite my soul," wrote Walt Whitman. "I contradict myself? Very well then, I contradict myself. (I am large. I contain multitudes.)"

If you act differently with different people, it doesn't mean you're a hypocrite. It means you're finding out who you are. Which takes time. Dave Matthews sings, "Am I right side up or upside down?"

Answer: Right side up. Honest.

*I am discovering who I am.*

*I still believe that at any time, the no-talent police*
*will come and arrest me.*

—Mike Myers

❀

Goethe wrote, "Know thyself? If I knew myself, I'd run away." Everyone has moments of self-doubt. A person who never suffers from self-doubt may be insufferable. But to constantly second-guess or berate or feel sorry for yourself is not ideal, either. "Self-pity in its early stages is as snug as a feather mattress," said Oprah Winfrey. "Only when it hardens does it become uncomfortable."

Forgive yourself for not being perfect, then strive to shore up your shortcomings. Can you be more considerate, more hard-working? Can you step out from behind the curtain and realize your potential?

Dorothy Parker wrote:

*I shall stay the way I am*
*Because I do not give a damn.*

Good poem; bad attitude. A little effort goes a long way. And if you start out apathetic, you can wind up pathetic.

**Step by step, I can move forward.**

*This little light of mine, I'm gonna let it shine.*

—*African American spiritual*

❀

If you put yourself down, others will follow. If you believe in yourself, others will follow.

When you strut your stuff, you're not being a show-off. You're making a contribution. Sharing your gifts. It takes courage to get out of your own way and run with your talents. Courage to excel in something. But don't you owe it to yourself to succeed? To make yourself proud?

Architect Frank Lloyd Wright said, "Early in life I had to choose between honest arrogance and hypocritical humility. I chose honest arrogance."

Don't be obnoxious. But do be amazing. Marianne Williamson wrote, "We ask ourselves, who am I to be brilliant, gorgeous, talented, and fabulous? Actually, who are you not to be? Your playing small doesn't serve the world. There is nothing enlightened about shrinking so that other people won't feel insecure around you. As we let our own light shine, we unconsciously give other people permission to do the same."

**I will shine.**

*The real fault is to have faults and not amend them.*

—*Confucius*

❀

A Hindu proverb says, "There is nothing noble about being superior to some other person. The true nobility is in being superior to your previous self." How have you grown this year? (Besides in height.) What have you learned in school? (Besides some history.) Have you taken a step forward in athletics or academics or art? Or have you learned, perhaps, that when you argue, your words have more impact if spoken quietly?

"Criticism," wrote Eleanor Roosevelt, "makes very little dent upon me, unless I think there is some real justification and something should be done." If a jerk insults you, shrug it off. Why let a jerk bring you down? But if someone you admire points out that you could have done better, don't let the words just hurt you. Let them teach you, inspire you.

Criticism stings most when you recognize truth in it. Yet in everybody and everything there is room for improvement. Instead of being defensive, reach higher, work harder.

We are all works in progress.

**Thoughtful criticism can be a favor in disguise.**

*I wish women would be proud of their bodies and
not diss other women for being proud of theirs.*
—Christina Aguilera

❀

Are you too critical? Do you routinely find fault in friends'
bodies or clothes or hair or taste in boys? Do you flip through
magazines and point our how terrible everyone looks, or
channel surf and comment on how stupid everyone sounds?
It's good to develop style and standards, not good to make
cynicism your specialty.

Molière cautioned, "One should examine oneself for a
very long time before thinking of condemning others."

In *The Portrait of a Lady* by Henry James, Isabel Archer
defends her friend: "It is very easy to laugh at her, but it is
not as easy to be as brave as she." Exactly. It's a cinch to
poke fun at someone in the spotlight, a challenge to step
into the glare yourself. So why not be generous? You don't
have to give a standing ovation to everyone who wears a
new outfit or makes a speech or sings a solo or writes an
editorial. But why be mean-spirited—unless you would
have others judge *you* that harshly?

Winston Churchill's mother, Jennie Jerome Churchill,
wrote, "Treat your friends as you do your pictures, and place
them in their best light."

**Supportive beats sarcastic.**

*I don't know the key to success,*
*but the key to failure is trying to please everybody.*
—*Bill Cosby*

❀

A Danish proverb warns: "He who builds according to every man's advice will have a crooked house."

Try to please yourself—not the indifferent popular group or your fickle friends or your impatient boyfriend or your unreasonable father.

"I was raised to sense what someone wanted me to be, and be that kind of person," actress Sally Fields recalls. "It took me a long time not to judge myself through someone else's eyes."

It is tempting to let others judge you, tempting to ask, "What do you think?" as you put on an outfit or sketch a portrait or play a tune. And true experts can offer valuable guidance. Yet many classmates and grown-ups know less than you do about your field of interest. So don't listen to them. Listen to the YES inside yourself. Give yourself a green light. As Tina Fey put it, "Saying yes allows you to move forward."

*If I do things their way, who will do things my way?*

*It might have been a hard thing for me
in high school or junior high, not being the prom queen
or whatever. But I know for certain that God made us
the way we're supposed to be, and I love everything
about myself, the way I look, my nose, my skin.*

—*India.Arie*

Do you like your looks? Can you learn to appreciate your reflection instead of picking yourself apart?

Some girls choose to have surgery in order to change their silhouettes. But isn't it better to make peace with your own body rather than voluntarily go under a knife?

Try to love your profile, your skin color, your eyes, your size.

You're small on top? Great!

You're big on top? Great!

You're fair, you're dark, you're blond, you're brunette, you're tall, you're petite?

It's all good.

Staying fit and healthy is important. Looking a particular way is not. Besides, there are a million ways to be beautiful.

As Margaret Wolfe Hungerford said, "Beauty is in the eye of the beholder."

**Behold! I look great!**

*I take care of myself because I learned early on that*
*I'm the only person who's responsible for me.*
—*Halle Berry*

❀

Are you taking good care of yourself, body and soul, inside and outside? Buddha said, "To keep the body in good health is a duty." He may have had a spare tire, but he was right about the importance of health.

"The field that has rested gives a beautiful crop," wrote Ovid. "There is a time for many words, and there is also a time for sleep," said Homer (the poet, not the *Simpsons* character). It is hard to turn off the lights when life feels full, but getting enough sleep is one key to staying healthy and happy. If you drink cola with dinner, then stay up until dawn, chatting on-line, you'll be wiped out the next day. Instead, snuggle into bed with or without a book. They say breaking up is hard to do, but waking up can be even harder—especially when you're sleep-deprived.

Get exercise, too. Whether you run, bicycle, skate, Rollerblade, or snowboard, whether you work out alone or with a team, staying fit means staying healthy. "Nothing lifts me out of a bad mood better than a hard workout," wrote Cher.

*I have only one body. I had better take care of it.*

*At thirteen, I thought more about my acne*
*than I did about God or world peace.*

—*Mary Pipher*

❦

You get to make a first impression only once. Yet just when you want to look your most dazzling, you have to contend with pimples or braces or the awkwardness of maturing more quickly or slowly than your friends. Everyone feels insecure at this age—especially the people who boast the most. The challenge is to smile as you make it through the obstacle course of adolescence.

Ben Folds sings, "Everybody knows it hurts to grow up." Always has, always will, because these are years of fast changes and roller-coaster mood swings.

But enthusiasm makes you attractive no matter what your skin, teeth, or body is up to. So don't fixate on the physical. And take comfort: Acne is not a losing battle, because you win in the end. Very soon, all your classmates will be more mature—their bodies *and* their behavior.

*I don't notice everyone else's new zits;*
*why would they notice mine?*

*I think women see me on the cover of magazines and
think I never have a pimple or bags under my eyes.
You have to realize that that's after two hours
of hair and makeup, plus retouching.
Even I don't wake up looking like Cindy Crawford.*
——Cindy Crawford

❦

You can try to look your best. You can wash your hair and brush your teeth. You can choose to apply makeup. You can wear clothes with flair. But be reasonable. In real life, even supermodels don't look like supermodels. And since you probably don't expect to sing as well as your favorite musician or run as fast as your favorite athlete, why despair just because you and a cover girl don't look like twins separated at birth?

"Good posture is the one thing anybody can do now to look better," wrote Helen Gurley Brown, who started *Cosmopolitan* magazine. Zeal and confidence really do matter more than perfect hair or perfect skin.

Stand tall, smile, and repeat after Maria in *West Side Story*: "I feel pretty, oh so pretty . . ."

In the long run, personality trumps appearance.

**When I feel good, I look good.**

*I didn't belong as a kid, and that always bothered me.*
*If only I'd known that one day my differences*
*would be an asset, then my early life*
*would have been much easier.*
—Bette Midler

❀

It's hard to feel awesome when you feel awkward. But hang in there. Believe in yourself; befriend yourself; be patient.

Remember *The Ugly Duckling*? Remember the happy ending? "He thought of how he had been taunted and tormented, and now he heard all of them saying that he was the most beautiful of all beautiful birds," wrote Hans Christian Andersen.

Jennifer Aniston said that at fashion shows, "I feel like a bit of an outsider. Everyone is looking you up and down. It reminds me of high school, when I was always the girl who wore the big black skirts because I was a little chunkier and that's all I could wear."

Comedian John Leguizamo said, "I was a nerd in junior high. A really bad nerd . . . I was the Quasimodo of Jackson Heights."

You can't skip adolescence. But you *will* get through it.

*I won't just be self-conscious.*
*I will be conscious of my self.*

*No one can pull the wool over my eyes. Cashmere,*
*maybe, but wool, never.*
—*Thurston Howell III of* Gilligan's Island

❀

What do your clothes say about you? Gilda Radner joked, "I base most of my fashion taste on what doesn't itch." Clothes don't have to be new or name brand. Why not wear what makes you feel comfortable, whether that means chic, laid-back, or a mix? Slowly, slowly dare to wear clothes that help tell people who you are.

Ralph Lauren said, "We all have to fight to maintain our own unique style and taste in a world that would have us conform." If you like the way someone looks, ask yourself why. Train your eye and experiment with jewelry, accessories, fabrics, color. "There is no such thing as an ugly woman—there are only the ones who do not know how to make themselves attractive," said Christian Dior. So don't just cover up or show skin. Think about the signals your clothes send.

**I can put color in my life.**

*On the way to school and on the way back,*
*we always passed the sweet shop. No we didn't,*
*we never passed it. We always stopped.*
*—Roald Dahl*

❀

We all love candy and cookies, but it's healthier to be fit than fat. Miguel de Cervantes, author of *Don Quixote*, was the first to ask, "Can we ever have too much of a good thing?" When it comes to food, the answer is yes. Being comfortable with yourself and your size is an important goal. But constant overeating may mean that something is "eating" you. Don't let greedy corporations and their nonstop advertising persuade you to guzzle fattening sodas and inhale junk food. Too many Americans are obese.

Many girls get obsessed by weight. But although eating too much can make you chubby, eating too little is just as bad. Skipping meals leaves you hungry and deprives your body of necessary energy and nutrients. And starving yourself or throwing up on purpose is dangerous. Rather than count calories or go on wacky diets or hop on the scale each day, cut back on Sweets, Seconds, Snacks, and Soda, and eat sensible balanced meals. Don't let food run—or ruin—your life. Food is fuel. You need it, but in moderation. Said Ben Franklin, "To lengthen thy life, lessen thy meals."

**Eating healthfully shows self-respect.**

*Manners are the happy way of doing things.*

—Ralph Waldo Emerson

❀

Emerson also said, "Your manners are always under examination, and are awarding or denying you very high prizes when you least think of it."

You may grumble when your grandmother says, "Napkin on your lap" or "Elbows off the table" or "Start with the outside fork," but people do notice your manners—as much as your appearance. Even cavemen munching mastodons probably followed some sort of protocol.

Have you heard this poem by Gelett Bergess?

> *The Goops they lick their fingers,*
> *And the Goops they lick their knives;*
> *They spill their broth on the tablecloth—*
> *Oh, they lead disgusting lives!*
> *The Goops they talk while eating,*
> *And loud and fast they chew;*
> *And that is why I'm glad that I*
> *Am not a Goop—are you?*

Sure, it's impressive that your best friend's big brother can burp the alphabet. But it doesn't exactly make you want to go out with him, does it?

**Manners matter.**

*Women understand the world more than men,*
*therefore they weep more often.*
——*The Kabbalah*

❀

Women are strong. "Though the sex to which I belong is considered weak," Queen Elizabeth I wrote a long time ago, "you will nevertheless find me a rock that bends to no wind." Now more than ever, thanks to the work of those who came before us, women can vote, make decisions, pursue careers, and enjoy the same rights and options as men. Are women and men the same? No. But, as the French say, *"Vive la différence."*

Women derive much of their strength from their keen awareness of relationships as well as goals. "True strength is delicate," wrote sculptor Louise Nevelson.

"Women observe subconsciously a thousand little details," said Agatha Christie. "And they call the result intuition."

There may be times when you will feel that you are being treated unfairly. Defend yourself. Speak your mind. You can be powerful *and* feminine.

**So I cried—**
**it's better to be sensitive than unfeeling.**

*Excellence is the best deterrent to racism or sexism.*

—Oprah Winfrey

❁

If you think you're being slighted because of your sex, race, or background, you have legitimate grounds for complaint. But don't make the victim card your ace in the hole. A better approach is to pour your energy into doing your best. When you triumph, you not only come out ahead, you also have the pleasure of proving skeptics wrong.

You are writing your own "personal suspense novel," said Mary Higgins Clark. "The plot is what you will do for the rest of your life, and you are the protagonist." Why not give your story character, adventure, and a heroine who is unstoppable?

"If you are going to think black, think positive about it," wrote opera singer Leontyne Price. "Don't think down on it, or think it is something in your way. This way, when you really want to stretch out, and express how beautiful black is, everybody will hear you."

Mel Brooks said, "Don't tap the bell. Ring the bell."

*Being an individual means taking pride in my differences, my similarities, my strengths.*

*Where you lead, I will follow.*

—*Carole King*

꧁

Are you a leader or a follower or a bit of both? Steamrollers get their way—but they crush everything in their path. Followers do what the group does—but they may notice later that they've been led astray. If you are savvy and can think for yourself, you can sometimes follow other people's trails and sometimes leave a trail of your own.

Whom would you be willing to follow? Some lucky girls find mentors—teachers or older classmates who can guide them toward interesting summers or promising careers. Less lucky girls can fall in with the wrong crowd—and wind up smoking, drinking, or worse. In the Bible, the apostle Matthew said, "If the blind lead the blind, both shall fall in the ditch."

If someone offers you cigarettes or beer or drugs, can you say no? If any group urges you to surrender your independence in order to belong, can you move on to a group where your opinions and your individuality are respected? Never get in the backseat if you don't know where you're going.

*If it doesn't feel right, it might be wrong.*

*Smoking is a custom loathsome to the eye, hateful to the nose, harmful to the brain, dangerous to the lungs.*

—King James I

❀

The newspapers keep reporting new studies that link smoking and disease. Duh! It's not news that smoking is bad news. England's King James I figured that one out four centuries ago!

Why start smoking? It's unhealthy, addictive, smelly, expensive, and in many places, against the law. And while a few people may think you're cool if you light up, a lot of others— girls and guys—will think less of you. Cigarettes can make many would-be friendships and romances go up in smoke.

What do you do if someone offers you a puff at the bus stop or in the girls' room? Don't offer an anti-tobacco lecture. Just decline. If you want, you can say that you don't like the taste or that smoking gives you a headache or that you're allergic. The point is not to start smoking. It makes your clothes smell and your teeth yellow and your lungs black and your breath gross. It can cause diseases that can kill you. It costs hundreds of dollars a year. And it's a very hard habit to break.

**Smoking? <u>So</u> not worth it.**

*I capped the bottle. I became conscious.*
*I was aware. It was time.*
—Al Pacino

❁

What if you have a friend who swills a beer at a party and wants you to drink, too? It can be hard to say no to a friend. But saying no to them can mean saying yes to yourself.

Drinking can be dangerous. Drinking can lead you to do something you'll later regret. Mixing drinks or drinking too much can make you throw up or pass out. Driving while drunk can cause a fatal accident. Never, ever, drive drunk—and never, ever, let someone who is drunk drive you anywhere. Call home or a taxi or a friend's parent. Do not risk your life because you're too embarrassed to speak up.

Just because your friend is drinking doesn't mean you have to. You don't have to report her or lecture her or dump her. Just take care of your own body and health. Don't go against your better judgment. By protecting yourself, you're also providing positive peer pressure. Gertrude Stein wrote, "It is so much more exciting to be exact and concentrated and sober." Nancy Astor wrote, "One reason I don't drink is I want to know when I'm having a good time."

*I don't have to drink to have fun.*

*All dope can do for you is kill you . . .*
*the long hard way. And it can kill the people*
*you love right along with you.*
—Billie Holiday

❁

Do you know someone on drugs? Do you feel respect for her? Or do you feel sorry for her?

Many older teens and adults have self-destructive habits. They smoke and find it's hard to quit. They drink and don't know when enough is enough. They do drugs and stop paying attention to their work or friends or family. Their habits are bad for them and can be dangerous to those who love them, especially if they make irresponsible decisions while drunk or high.

The easiest way to avoid getting addicted to a drug or getting busted by the police is to stay away from drugs in the first place. You don't need them. So don't run the risk of getting kicked out of school or sent to prison or to an emergency room. When life is hard, don't be hard on yourself, and don't do things that will make matters worse.

**I can be self-constructive, not self-destructive.**

*The plant is blind but it knows enough to keep pushing*
*upwards towards the light, and it will do this*
*in the face of endless discouragements.*
—George Orwell

If you keep forging ahead, you get where you are going. If you keep moving despite the odds and obstacles, you win. And when you do encounter hard times? Have faith that life gets easier once you get the hang of it. Experience teaches perspective; peace comes after pain; triumph can follow defeat.

"I think these difficult times have helped me to understand better than before, how infinitely rich and beautiful life is in every way," wrote Isak Dinesen, "and that so many things that one goes around worrying about are of no importance whatsoever."

To see the bigger picture, step back. That can help you distinguish major troubles from minor ones. You didn't get invited to a party? That hurts—but you still have friends. You missed an easy shot in basketball? Bummer—but you're still a good player. You have too much homework? A drag—but hey, you have food, shelter, and people who love you.

*When I step back, big problems look smaller.*

*Two roads diverged in the wood, and I—*
*I took the one less traveled by,*
*And that has made all the difference.*

—Robert Frost

❀

Indira Gandhi said, "The beaten track does not lead to new pastures." Take the time you need to find yourself and to find your path, your track. You know how different you are from your friends, family and neighbors. Your passions are different, as are your successes and setbacks. Even what makes you laugh or cry may be different.

"Go confidently in the direction of your dreams!" wrote Henry David Thoreau. "Live the life you've imagined." He also wrote, "If a man does not keep pace with his companions, perhaps it is because he hears a different drummer."

Can you someday take charge, not orders? Answer to yourself. Heed the *Star Trek* advice "to boldly go where no one has gone before." After all, if you follow the crowd, you might get lost in it. Garry Trudeau, the *Doonesbury* cartoonist, said, "Surprise yourselves. Surprise your parents. Surprise the world."

*I won't follow footsteps; I'll make tracks.*

# ❀
# *Friendship*

*Girlfriends . . . they keep me sane.*

—*Jennifer Aniston*

❀

There's nothing like good friends. They congratulate and console. They offer a sympathetic ear and a second opinion. They provide company and merriment. And they help you feel good about yourself.

You don't need one particular best friend, and you don't need to be popular. But you do need a real friend or two. As Francis Bacon put it, "Without friends, the world is but a wilderness."

Learning to be friendly and to befriend others is every bit as important as academic learning. Some girls make the mistake of competing with their friends or of becoming possessive or jealous of them. Others twist themselves into knots trying to win popularity contests. Others retreat behind shyness and live lonely lives.

Are you likeable? Do you have friends now and friends for life?

*If life is cake, friendship is frosting.*

*My friends are my estate.*

—Emily Dickinson

❁

You're stuck with your relatives, but you can *choose* your friends. Whenever you find yourself wishing you could be friends with someone, ask yourself why. Is it because that person is pretty or popular? Or is it because you and she share common ground?

With a friend, you can think aloud and talk freely and comfortably without always having to explain everything. She listens with interest and without teasing.

If you live to run, find a friend who wants to discuss times, tracks, and shin splints. If you love English, find a friend who wants to trade books and literary opinions or start a book club. If you've weathered your parents' divorce, consider confiding in someone whose parents have also broken up. Look for girls who share the same passions, problems, and pastimes you do. Look for girls who are friendly, smart, and kind, and who like to talk about guys, TV, music, movies, politics, websites, whatever. "Talk is a refuge," said Zora Neale Hurston.

*I will think about whom I want to be friends with and why.*

*The only way to have a friend is to be one.*

—Ralph Waldo Emerson

❀

To make friends, get involved. Join the basketball team or French club or student government or literary magazine, and meet others who share your interests. Then say hello (even if you're feeling shy) and introduce yourself. Ask questions, laugh approvingly, smile, listen well, and keep secrets.

People like people who like them. If you seem warm and interested, girls and guys will respond to you. If you say nothing, you may come off as cold and distant even if you're only timid.

Be visible and vibrant, cheerful and curious. You'll make more friends than if you spend your days inside peering wistfully out the window. Though everybody feels nervous at times, if you break through your shell you're doing yourself and those around you a favor. So try to relax. As Anne Lamott wrote, "Don't look at your feet to see if you're doing it right. Just dance."

*I will get to know people;*
*I will let them get to know me.*

*Time spent laughing is time spent with the gods.*

—*Japanese proverb*

Do you know girls who are fun and funny? Who think positive and love to laugh? It's hard not to like a good sport who enjoys a good time.

Being serious and earnest is admirable. Being whiny and complaining is trouble.

"Whoever is happy will make others happy, too," wrote Anne Frank. Moods are contagious. If someone is full of energy, it lifts you up. If someone is bitter, it pulls you down. So cultivate your sense of fun. Save the somber heart-to-hearts for those who already love you. As an African proverb puts it: "Sorrow is like a precious treasure shown only to friends." Friends, mind you. Not girls you just met and hope to know better.

**Better sweet than sour.**

*You can make more friends in two months by becoming
interested in other people than you can in two years
by trying to get other people interested in you.*
—Dale Carnegie

❀

Want to make friends? Make it your mission to help others feel comfortable and confident and interesting. One way to jump-start a friendship is to talk about someone's interests. Ask what movies or music or magazines or books she likes. Has your classmate taken the time to put together a portfolio or scrapbook or to master the violin or a computer game? What would happen if you said "You're amazing!" rather than "Let's watch TV"? If you recognize and appreciate someone's talent, that person is likely to take note of your talents, too. Even if you simply ask, "How was your weekend?" before detailing the highlights of yours, that person will confide and listen with added interest.

"If therefore, there be any kindness I can show," wrote William Penn, founder of Pennsylvania, the state of brotherly love, "let me do it now, and not defer or neglect it, as I shall not pass this way again."

*The more generous I am with others,
the more generous they may be with me.*

*What I cannot love, I overlook. Is that real friendship?*

—*Anaïs Nin*

❀

You may not like or agree with every word your friends say. Or you may adore them—yet not understand one's passion for rap or another's indifference to politics. "The art of being wise," wrote William James, "is the art of knowing what to overlook." George Santayana said, "Friendship is always the union of part of one mind with part of another; people are friends in spots."

Do you have more than one close friend? You and one girl may like to bake together. You and a second may like to play sports. You and a third may like to practice Spanish while discussing boys. *(Sí, es guapo. Es muy guapo.)* It's good to have more than one friend because different friends bring out your different qualities, and because girls move and girls change. Besides, too much togetherness can make twosomes tiresome. Can you enjoy your friends without closing yourself off to the rest of the class? Can you manage not to mind when your friends hang out with other girls or with each other? Remember that you and your friends like each other—you don't own each other, and you don't need to mirror each other.

**I can't get it all from one friend.**

*I get by with a little help from my friends.*

*—Ringo Starr*

❁

A German proverb says, "Friendship is a plant that one must often water." Sometimes you'll want to talk about family, school, boys. A good friend will be there. Sometimes your friend will need to talk and it will be your turn to listen, no matter how busy you are. If you take care of your friendships, the best ones can last for years. If you dump your friends when a more popular person shows up, or when your crush asks you out, your friendships will be long gone when you are looking for company or comfort. Sure, you'll make new friends. But there's nothing like an old friend.

Without water, flowers dry up, and without attention, friendships fade. But just as too much water can kill plants, too much attention can drive friends away. Neither ignore nor smother friends. Like you, they need room to be themselves and to reach out to others.

You know how *you* feel. Make an effort to switch camera angles from time to time to see the world from your friend's point of view. It's okay to take, but you have to give, too.

**No one cares how much I know unless they know how much I care.**

*Never look down on anybody unless*
*you're helping them up.*
—*Jesse Jackson*

❀

Be open-minded, not narrow-minded. Give the new girl in school a chance. Smile back to that friendly kid in chorus. Keep up with your best buddy from fourth grade even if the popular group dismisses her. Don't judge by looks alone.

Try to find what you like in someone, not what you dislike. A particular girl annoys you? Don't hang out with her. But don't whisper about her or make fun of her. ("We are not amused," England's Queen Victoria said royally when she caught a staff member imitating her.)

According to the apostle Matthew, Jesus said, "Judge not that ye be not judged." Next time classmates are being snide or mean about an acquaintance or friend, consider discouraging them. Say, "C'mon. Give her a break," or "He's not all that bad," or even, "You'd like her if you got to know her."

Rejecting people without giving them a chance is shortsighted. And besides, as Colette said, "What a delight it is to make friends with someone you have despised."

**I will not make every day Judgment Day.**

*I don't have girlfriends who are inconsiderate to other women. It's all about taking care of each other.*

—Cameron Diaz

❁

Sure you wanted to win the school raffle. But what if your friend has the winning stub? Congratulate her. Later, when you win a contest or give a speech, she will cheer or root for you—rather than hope you mess up or seethe in secret.

Jealousy is natural. If your friend's room is jazzier than yours, you're bound to notice. But don't dwell on what she has; focus on what you have. Instead of being competitive, work to feel proud of and to outdo yourself. And know that even winners have troubles. No one really has it made. Satisfaction is never guaranteed.

According to the Bhagavad Gita, "Hell has three gates: lust, anger, and greed." Imagine your neighbor's family just bought a cool new car, or your ex-best friend has a great new boyfriend. You can fume about how she doesn't deserve it, and obsess about you versus her. Or you can break free and move on.

"If you're going to hold someone down," Toni Morrison wrote, "you're going to have to hold on by the other end of the chain."

*I will build myself up rather than put myself or my friends down.*

*I praise loudly; I blame softly.*

—*Queen Catherine II*

❀

Flattery will get you nowhere? Ha! "Flattery'll get you anywhere," Jane Russell's character said in *Gentlemen Prefer Blondes*. Flattery is always welcome and is a great way to break the ice and make new friends.

When you don't know what to say to a girl, boy, or grown-up, pay a compliment like: "You draw so well" or "Great scarf" or "Your field goal was incredible." Everyone likes to be praised, so why not praise in public?

How are you at accepting compliments? If someone says, "I like your sweater," do you answer, "This gross thing? I got it at the Salvation Army"? How does that make her feel? What if, instead, you just said "Thanks"?

You should be loud and lavish with praise, but if you criticize, keep it quiet and private. Think about this Jamaican saying: "When you point your finger at another person, look at where the other fingers point." And this line from the first page of *The Great Gatsby*: "Whenever you feel like criticizing someone, just remember that all the people in this world have not had the advantages that you've had."

*I will compliment at least one person every day.*

*I learned to write a lot of thank-you notes*
*and to be gracious. I think that has helped me in*
*the business—just being courteous and caring.*
—*Reese Witherspoon*

❀

Parents are more apt to say, "Why don't you invite Julia for dinner?" if Julia often says please and thank-you. But even kids notice manners and social skills.

If you're saying hi to a bunch of friends, and Rachel walks over, instead of turning your back on her, open the circle and welcome her in. Say, "Hi. We were just talking about the gymnastics meet." Or, "You guys know Rachel, right?" What if you were about to mention that Michael—the guy who dumped Rachel—just asked out Emma? Have a heart. Save that tidbit for later.

Always consider other people's feelings and perspectives. Don't say, "I'm glad I'm not an only child" if she is, or "My room is so small" if hers is half the size, or "Can't wait till the party" if she wasn't invited. Being polite is not a way to scam adults. It's a way to live life more smoothly.

**Better to build bridges than to burn them.**

*It was a delightful visit . . .*
*perfect in being much too short.*
—*Jane Austen*

❀

You've heard that guests and fish smell after three days? Sometimes it's even sooner.

Be a good guest—a friend, not a freeloader. Don't eat someone out of house and home. Don't appear at someone's door uninvited every afternoon. Don't reserve a permanent seat in front of a friend's computer or television.

Sleeping at a friend's? Don't assume it's okay to spend the whole next day there, too. You and your friend will probably wake up tired, and so will her parents. Quit while you're ahead, and once you're home, don't race to the phone to catch up on your moments apart.

Joining a family for a weekend or holiday? Be helpful and polite and don't expect to be entertained every minute. Help with dishes. Give a present. (Cookies you bake? Photos you take?) Say thank you at the end of your stay. Warning: The longer you put off writing a thank-you note, the better it has to be.

**I won't wear out my welcome.**

*There is only one thing in the world worse than being talked about, and that is not being talked about.*
*—Oscar Wilde*

❀

When you leave the table in the lunchroom or get out of the car after soccer practice, you may hope that your left-behind friends don't say anything about you. And they may not. Chances are, your complexion or your poor grade or your mother's ugly shoes are a bigger deal in your mind than in theirs. You may wave farewell and they may go right on talking about birthdays or baby-sitting, movies or math tests.

But if the girls do discuss you, that's not so terrible. You talk about others, and other will talk about you. They might say something nice. Or someone might diss you while another defends you. Or someone may be jealous and express envy as contempt.

Being talked about is a small price to pay for being visible. Instead of hoping that everyone stays silent if your name comes up, hope that not too many people have to stop and ask, "Who's she?"

*I don't like everybody.*
*Everybody doesn't have to like me.*

*Whoever gossips to you will gossip about you.*

—*Lebanese proverb*

❀

Everybody gossips a little. As Barbara Walters said, "Show me someone who never gossips, and I'll show you someone who isn't interested in people." Gossip can bind friendships, clarify thoughts, and help you figure out where you fit in.

But gossiping can go too far, and some people can't resist badmouthing friends as well as strangers. Ben Franklin quipped, "To find out a girl's faults, praise her to her girlfriends." Is that true in your circle?

If you're laughing as one of your friends trashes another's clothes, handwriting, or taste in boys, know that when your back is turned she may open fire on you—or convert your big problems into her small talk. A girl who casually spreads rumors or breaches confidences is not to be trusted. So think before you bare your soul. And next time a person puts down someone you like, instead of laughing, defend her. At the very least, don't report back to the maligned friend. Don't relay hurtful insults in the name of higher truth. If you say, "Jessica told me she hates the way you dress," you're not being refreshingly candid. You're being as cruel as Jessica.

**Those who engage in sharp-edged gossip often get cut.**

*Honesty is the best policy.*

—*Aesop*

❀

Aesop's fables are wonderful to read and reread, and they teach a lot about right and wrong. But Aesop must have known that honesty is not *always* the best policy. You should strive to be honest with friends, parents, yourself. But use your judgment. Unless a situation is dangerous, tattling is rarely worth it.

A wise person knows when to say the truth instead of what someone hopes to hear and when to say what someone hopes to hear instead of the truth. In a store, for instance, it's okay to say, "I wouldn't buy those pants—they seem a bit snug." But if you're already in school when a girl asks, "Do these pants look okay?" the best answer is probably "Yes."

Somerset Maugham wrote, "People ask you for criticism, but they only want praise." So be tactful. White lies have their place, and there's no need to start sentences with "No offense, but . . ."

**I can be thoughtful as well as truthful.**

*The day we see the truth and cease to speak*
*is the day we begin to die.*
——*Martin Luther King, Jr.*

❀

Truth is tricky. You probably wouldn't—and shouldn't—report an overheard insult or tell a friend that you can't stand her parents. But there are times when you must tell the truth, when disclosure beats discretion. If your best friend has a boyfriend, and you sometimes feel excluded, that's no reason to badmouth him. But what if she confesses that her boyfriend hits her? What if a close friend who is always dieting reveals that she hardly eats anything at all anymore? What if a friend who is often depressed says she's cutting herself or thinking about killing herself? What should you do?

Speak up! It may seem easier to stay mum, but is it easy to swallow your words day after day? And how would you feel if something terrible happened? Tell your friend you respect and love her and that you're worried about her. Confide in a trusted adult (parent, teacher, counselor, member of the clergy) to get her more help and information. In such cases, you're not betraying her confidence. You may be saving her life.

**Good friends speak up.**

*Friendship is one eye closed, one eye opened.*

——*Chinese proverb*

Just because you offer your friend good advice doesn't mean she's going to take it. You can tell her that cupcakes and cigarettes make a lousy lunch, but that doesn't mean she's going to sit down tomorrow with soup, salad, and milk. You can say that she's getting a reputation as a flirt, but that doesn't mean she's going to change her ways by Wednesday. And you can confess that you don't see what she sees in her greaseball of a boyfriend, but that doesn't mean she'll tell him it's over.

Despite your offer of sage advice, a friend may keep right on skipping lunch, skipping class, or worse. If her life or her health is in jeopardy, you can pipe up one more time or talk with your parent or a trusted adult. But if the situation is not dangerous, let matters go. It's her life, not yours. You may decide to become less close to her. Or you may decide that it's okay if you and a friend have different attitudes toward smoking, boys, school, everything.

*I can choose my friends but I can't change them.*

*Avoid popularity if you would have peace.*

—*Abraham Lincoln*

❀

When asked what magic power she would choose for herself, author J.K. Rowling said, "It would be the power of invisibility." After all, she is so popular that now it's hard for her to cross the street in peace.

Lots of girls yearn to be more popular. But who are the girls who really care about you? Do you have a friend you can call when you are excited—or upset? Do you have different friends who bring out your different interests? Do you feel free to be with whomever you want, boy or girl? If so, count yourself lucky.

Yes, the handful of popular kids may be pleased that the masses have empowered them. But some popular kids feel boxed in. Some feel pressured to act happy all the time. Some want to hang with former friends, but are afraid to be seen with girls who aren't "in," even though they feel sad (and guilty) about letting old friendships slip away.

If *you* are popular, enjoy the advantages, but stay kind and sensitive. If you are not popular, try not to dwell on one small knot of girls, especially if they aren't giving you a thought. Instead, keep meeting new people and appreciating true friends.

**A friend is worth more than a fan club.**

*I wasn't a geek exactly: I was more of a bookworm.*

—Kristin Kreuk

❦

Shakespeare wrote, "Reputation is an idle and most false imposition; oft got without merit, and lost without deserving." When it comes to reputations, school can be particularly rough. How come your neighbor is in the cool group while there's a rumor going around about you? "Life," as David Letterman put it, "ain't all gum and root beer." When everyone knows everyone else's business, and everyone swims in the same puny fishbowl, it's hard to change your image. But it's still doable. (Rumors are short-lived—and you shouldn't believe all you hear, either!)

If you kowtow to popular kids, desperate to penetrate their circle, your sense of self goes down the tubes. Says a Creole proverb: "Make yourself a floor mat and people will wipe their feet on you." Are you okay with who you are? Great. If not, shake up your image. Be nice to kids outside your clique. Sign up for after-school activities and branch out even if people think of you as pure jock, brain, or artist. Dress in a way that is more (or less) eye-catching. Become an expert at something. IM someone new. Bottom line: you're driving your bus, so if you're stuck in a ditch, rev your engines and climb out!

**It's never too late to clean the slate.**

*Remember, no one can make you feel inferior*
*without your consent.*
——*Eleanor Roosevelt*

❀

Have you ever said, "He made me so mad" or "She makes me feel like a loser" or "The teacher made me feel stupid"? How can anyone really make you feel anything? They're your feelings. If a person you like acts aloof, that's disappointing. But why let her behavior toward you cast a shadow on your opinion of yourself? If certain people don't recognize your strengths, that's their loss. If your latest crush doesn't fall for you, he isn't rejecting you; he just isn't picking you out of the crowd.

How come that girl in homeroom is acting stuck up anyway? Is she insecure? Jealous? Is her home life hell? Did she not make cheerleader? Let her negative energy be her problem, not yours. Why feel the way she wants you to feel?

Do not give other people power over you. As Katie Couric says, "There are many people who will try to stand in your way, even cut you off at the knees for whatever reason, but it is often more about them than about you."

*If they can't tell I'm amazing,*
*they need new glasses.*

*The colander said to the needle,*

*"Get away, you have holes in you!"*

—Indian proverb

❀

Why does a particular girl drive you insane? Is it because she, like you, wants to be an excellent student or a phenomenal swimmer? Is she, like you, a little too concerned about how she measures up—physically and socially?

If someone bothers you, ask yourself why. It may have as much to do with you as it does with her. It's hard to watch someone strain to be popular or impress a teacher or attract a guy—if you know you've been there. Or perhaps she reminds you of your bossy sister, annoying cousin, or someone else you can't write out of your life. Or perhaps she brings out your competitive side. You want to be the fastest, brightest, best. Fine. It's natural to feel that way. But can you strive to outdo yourself, not just others?

Whenever you and someone else have qualities or interests in common, try to make that a recipe for friendship instead of rivalry or animosity. E. B. White wrote: "One of the most time-consuming things is to have an enemy."

**When I don't like someone, I can learn from it.**

*Help thyself, and God will help thee.*

*—Jean de La Fontaine*

❀

When La Fontaine penned these words, he was not—repeat, not—referring to shoplifting. If you ever find yourself in a group of girls who are starting to steal, drink, vandalize, harass others, or do anything that makes you cringe, think about speaking up or moving on. Why risk your health or break the law? Why do something that makes you uncomfortable? Why go where you don't want to go?

"Oh, c'mon, just take the mascara. Who's going to know?" Answer: You. You'll know. And possibly a store guard. And the police. And your parents.

You don't have to report your friends if you don't want to. You don't have to say a word. But if you say, "I don't want to steal [or drink or fight]," someone else in your group may admit that she doesn't want to either. There is such a thing as positive peer pressure.

There is also such a thing as reaching out to new friends. After all, by choosing to spend so much time with a certain girl or guy or group, you are choosing not to spend that time with other people—people who could become friends.

**If it's risky or wrong, I won't go along.**

*Lily smiled at her classification of her friends.*
*How different they had seemed to her a few hours ago!*
*Then they had symbolized what she was gaining,*
*now they stood for what she was giving up.*
—*Edith Wharton*

❀

Are your friends changing? Or is it you? Some friendships that are quickly made, quickly fade. Other friendships that started long ago fade away. "My friends don't seem to be friends at all but people whose phone numbers I haven't lost," a character muses in a Nick Hornby novel. If, week after week, you don't like your friends as much as you'd like to, it may be time to drift apart.

Say your tomboy friend becomes boy crazy, your horseback riding pal spikes her hair, and you have gotten heavy into hockey. You are all out of sync. As Lillian Hellman said, "People change and forget to tell each other." You don't have to be mean as you step away, and you shouldn't ditch a loyal friend who is going through a stressful time. (Why bite the hand that needs you?) But if you do want to expand your social horizons, you can.

It's your friend who's getting restless? Give her a little space. Everyone needs some breathing room.

*I don't need friends who don't need me.*

*Waste not fresh tears over old griefs.*

*—Euripides*

❀

You're slowly easing into a new clique—or at least bonding with a new girl. But you still miss your ex-best friend. It still hurts when you see her hanging out with that other girl in the hall or at the mall. You still remember the fun times you two had together—at your home, at slumber parties, in swimming pools, on Halloween, in front of her television and your computer, and when you went with her to get her ears pierced.

Of course you're sad! "When a lovely thing dies, smoke gets in your eyes." That's from a Jerome Kern song. (He wasn't talking cigarettes; he was talking tears.)

The fact that you're still hurting shows that you have a big heart and that you really cared about your friend. Go ahead and soak your pillow.

"I love crying," said Tom Wolfe. "It's one of the best ways of getting rid of the things that are going to haunt you." But after crying, dry your eyes and focus on today and on new friends, girls and guys. Join a team or the band or an after-school group. Get involved. "Action," wrote Joan Baez, "is the antidote to despair."

*When a friendship ends, I will grieve. But not forever.*

*Friendship is like money, easier made than kept.*

—Samuel Butler

❀

Friends move and friends change. But if you and another girl want to be close forever, there are ways to protect your friendship. And according to a Yiddish proverb, "One old friend is better than two new ones."

Can you stay in touch even during camp or vacation or if one of you moves? Can you telephone or exchange postcards, letters, or e-mail and IMs? Can you schedule visits? Don't get hung up on who owes whom a letter and how many pages it is. The point is to communicate, not to keep count.

If you and a friend have had a fight, can you find your way out of it? Were you displacing anger when you were actually mad at your gym teacher, not your friend? Even if that's not the case, try to work things out. Instead of saying, "Well, it was your fault!" try "Sorry I got mad." Or "I miss you and I want us to make up." Or "Come over; I bought rum raisin— your favorite." Or "Even Khaki the cocker spaniel has been wondering where you've been." Don't discard friendship. "It's easy to throw something into the river," goes a Kashmir saying, "but hard to take it out again."

*Better to lose an argument than to lose a friend.*

*Love*

*One word frees us of all the weight and pain of life:*
*That word is love.*

—*Sophocles*

❀

You feel like singing! You feel like dancing! You feel like sliding down the banister and hugging your cat and calling up the whole world! You look in the mirror and wink. Every lyric of every song on the radio is speaking to you. You can't wait to get to school, but as you dress, you daydream. You head to the bus stop, and the drizzle feels like sunshine. You marvel at the green of the trees and the scent of the air. You look at the flowers in your neighbor's garden and they seem gloriously, painfully, strikingly beautiful.

Could this be love?

Maybe. There's nothing as invigorating as love, especially when it's with a warm and wonderful person who loves you back. But take it slowly. One-way love can be frustrating, and you can drive yourself crazy over an impossible crush or spend years obsessing about someone who doesn't even know your name. Enjoy caring about a person, yes. But don't let love make you miserable.

*Falling in love is fun; stepping in is wise.*

*If love is the answer,*
*could you rephrase the question?*
—Lily Tomlin

❧

True or false: Everyone has a boyfriend except you. False.
Though couples are very visible in school and at the pool or
the park, most girls and guys have *not* paired off. Whether
you have or haven't, what's important is to feel whole even
when you are alone. You are not half a person waiting to be
completed. You are a whole person with thoughts and feelings you may be ready to share.

Friedrich Nietzsche wrote, "One must learn to love oneself . . . with a wholesome and healthy love, so that one can
bear to be with oneself and need not roam."

Love yourself and you seem friendly and likeable. Loathe
yourself and you seem needy and desperate. Everyone feels
lonely at times, but if you appreciate your own company and
are able to enjoy reading a book or writing in a journal or
taking a solitary walk, you'll be happier than if you depend
on constant companionship.

*I won't give all my love away;*
*I'll save some for myself.*

*Don't threaten me with love, baby.*
*Let's just go walking in the rain.*
—Billie Holiday

❀

Some girls hurl themselves headfirst into love. Others take their time before signing on with one person. It's wise to proceed with caution.

So don't tell someone you hardly know that you like him. And don't tell someone whom you only sort of like that you love him.

Just keep smiling and talking and flirting. The flirtation stage is fun and often less tricky and fragile than love. Why? Because once you give someone the power to make you happy, that person also has the power to hurt you— even without meaning to.

Be careful with your caring. Take things slowly. As Jorge Luis Borges warned, "To fall in love is to create a religion that has a fallible god."

**Having a boyfriend is not necessarily better**
**than having a crush.**

*Love is something sent from heaven*
*to worry the hell out of you.*
—*Dolly Parton*

❀

One of your classmates won't stop talking about a blue-eyed movie star. Another is hung up on the lead guitarist of a British band. Another is head over heels for the soccer coach or her best friend's boyfriend. Another is pumped about a boy she met at camp two summers ago even though he has ignored all her e-mails.

Though Cupid often misses his mark, some girls enjoy one-way romances. But others do not enjoy pining over passions that are out of reach, off-limits, or just plain hopeless. While it's not always possible to control feelings, most infatuations are like small flames. You can snuff them out or fan them into a fire. If a lopsided or forbidden romance is bumming you out, try to set yourself free. Then stay on the lookout for available guys who are worth your time and affection.

Changing crushes is not only permissible, it's instructive. "Falling out of love is very enlightening," wrote Iris Murdoch. "For a short while you see the world with new eyes."

**A boyfriend should also be a friend.**

*And if I loved you Wednesday, Well, what is that to you?*
*I do not love you Thursday—So much is true.*

—*Edna St. Vincent Millay*

✤

A new heartthrob every day may be a bit much, but you are entitled to change your mind about your feelings. You may like someone less as you get to know him more. Or you may give up on the crush who has never looked your way. Or you may find that it's the boy (or perhaps the girl) next door who puts a skip in your step.

That's okay. This is the time for learning about what draws you to a person.

Guys can be fickle, too. A Shakespeare song goes: "Sigh no more, ladies, sigh no more, men were deceivers ever; one foot in sea and one on shore; to one thing constant never."

Romance does not come with guarantees, and at this stage it's probably just as well. After all, changing your mind makes more sense than thinking about a guy who isn't thinking about you, or clinging to someone you no longer really like.

*Just because we like each other today doesn't mean*
*we should get married tomorrow.*

*If you want to be loved, be lovable.*

*—Ovid*

❀

What kind of guys catch your eye? Do they mumble and mope? Do they frown and scuff their feet and act colossally bored all the time? Probably not. Chances are they are energetic, good-looking, smart, and smiling. (Like you, right?)

If you're looking for romance, don't just hang out at home. Get involved with after-school activities and have fun as you find out what excites you and what you're good at. Theater? Sports? Politics? French? Science? Writing? Horses? Guitar? Cooking? Computer? Choir?

Winston Churchill wrote about "a modest little person, with much to be modest about." Don't let that describe you. How many great guys have you met while alone at home? (Cyberstrangers don't count.) It's while pursuing different activities that you are likely to meet someone interesting who is interested in pursuing you. And when you two do meet, will you be prickly, snobby? No way. As Arthur Guiterman wrote:

> The porcupine, whom one must handle gloved,
> May be respected, but is never loved.

**Lovable? C'est moi.**

*I love talking about nothing.*
*It's the only thing I know something about.*
—Oscar Wilde

❀

Lots of people get timid and tongue-tied. But if you can talk to girls, you can talk to guys. Try to be friendly (not flirty) and approachable (not locked in an impenetrable clique).

No crush? No problem. You can still have boy buddies. Think of boys as boys. Not as status symbols or intimidating members of the opposite sex.

What if someone you don't like likes you? Can you be nice without leading him on? He's got good taste, so why ridicule him? If he's not getting the message that his feelings aren't mutual, act aloof or, if necessary, let him down kindly. Tell him (privately) that you like him as a friend and are not looking to go out with anyone. Be gentle with bad news. As Cake sings, "To me, coming from you, friend is a four-letter word."

At first, romance may seem hit-or-miss. But you'll get better at figuring out whom you like and who likes you, and at figuring out how much of yourself to invest. It all starts with a hello and a smile.

**I will not die from saying hi.**

*Dreams are, by definition, cursed with short life spans.*

—*Candice Bergen*

❀

Just say a girl has her eye on a guy. She notices what he wears to school, where he sits at lunch, when he leaves which class, and how he gets home. She melts when he smiles and would give anything anything *anything* to go out with him.

Often, nothing happens. He doesn't single her out. He dates some other girl—her best friend, her worst enemy. But once every blue moon, the two become a couple.

Even then, things sometimes fizzle. Sure, many couples go the distance. But most students aren't meant to be each other's first and only love. Hard to believe, but a girl who has fixated on someone for months may find after the first exciting phone call that they have little to talk about. Or that their ideas and values are miles apart. Or perhaps they will go out for a month before she discovers that watching him fix his car or drum with his band isn't all that enthralling after all. Or that the longing and yearning were more intense than the official relationship.

**Some dreams, if realized, would be nightmares.**

*The average man is more interested in a woman
who is interested in him than he is in
a woman with beautiful legs.*
—*Marlene Dietrich*

❁

Show-stopping legs can grab a guy's attention. But to keep his attention—or win his heart—there must be a meeting of the minds.

Boys notice cute girls, but they fall for girls who laugh at their jokes, ask about their weekends, compliment their shirts or haircuts, and tune in to what they have to say. They like girls who like them (and like themselves).

It goes both ways. Have you noticed that boy with the biceps? Probably. More beguiling is the boy who has noticed you. The one who smiles and doesn't yawn or interrupt or walk away when you talk. The friendly one who pays attention to you on the phone rather than putting you on speaker phone as he also checks his e-mail or lifts weights or does his math.

If you are fixated on a boy who has a fan club, he may not notice one more admirer. If, however, you discover someone on your own, things may click. Perhaps someone who has been there all along?

*Half of love is listening.*

*The heart has its reasons which reason knows nothing of.*

*——Blaise Pascal*

❁

The Chinese have a saying: "One dog barks because it sees something; a hundred dogs bark because they heard the first dog bark." Sometimes the whole school seems to like one particular guy. Maybe you do, too.

Other times, you alone have fallen for the quiet foreign exchange student (your friends don't get it) or the class clown (your parents don't get it).

You can't always explain love—and you don't have to. You, not your peers or your parents, are the one with your feelings, and unless your guy is in jail, much older, or going out with your best friend, you don't need to justify your attraction. Even to him. If you two have fun together, talking and laughing, you don't have to pick apart your relationship. You can just relish it.

Mark Twain wrote, "You can't reason with your heart; it has its own laws and thumps about things which the intellect scorns."

**I will not analyze everything to death.**

*The great question . . . which I have not been able to answer despite my thirty years of research into the feminine soul, is "What does a woman want?"*
—Sigmund Freud

❀

Different women want different things. Attractiveness counts, sometimes even double, but most girls want a caring companion, a person who can accompany them to a concert or movie, a person who can cheer them on at a field hockey match or school play. Most look for a partner they like and respect and who likes and respects them.

In their rush to have boyfriends, however, some girls are reckless with their hearts. They forget that the point isn't just to get a guy but to built a wonderful relationship with a wonderful guy. Some girls settle too soon for someone selfish or unworthy. He's happy to kiss her, but he doesn't care about her cares.

Can you hang on to your self-respect and your standards as you think about who intrigues you and why? Can you be thoughtful with your heart?

*I will not shortchange myself.*

*The human race, in which so many of my readers belong, has been playing at children's games from the beginning, and will probably do it till the end, which is a nuisance for the few people who grow up.*

—G. K. Chesterton

❀

Romance is complicated enough without playing games or using go-betweens.

If you play hard to get, he may not be able to decode your scrambled signals. If you enlist a friend to test the waters, she may botch the job. What if she proclaims your undying love in front of the whole cafeteria? What if she jumbles up his heartfelt answer? What if she starts flirting with him herself?

Rather than play games, be direct. Don't *tell* him how you feel, *show* him. Don't put him on the spot with a point-blank "Do you like me?" Smile, talk, laugh, listen, compliment, ask questions, sit by him, look at him. And notice if he's smiling back and holding up his end of the conversation.

He is? Hurray! He's not? His loss. Accept this and move on. Who wants an unenthusiastic boyfriend anyway? And who wants a guy who doesn't know a gem (you!) when he sees one?

**I will show, not tell.**

*It's hard to find your true Prince Charming these days.*

—*Jennifer Lopez*

❀

Always has been. So before you announce that your new boyfriend is the cutest, funniest, smartest, and most talented person in the world, do a reality check. Is he perfect? Are you? Is anybody?

"Love involves a peculiar unfathomable combination of understanding and misunderstanding," wrote photographer Diane Arbus. The air between you is hypercharged. You sparkle extra for each other, and you make each other your top priority. You get along so well and you want him to accept you completely, so you decide he feels your every feeling, believes your every belief, and will be there forever. That's the magic of early love.

Then one day he hurts your feelings, or says something you disagree with, or is too busy to call. Does this mean he's a lout and your love is a sham? Or could it just mean that your initial expectations were unrealistic?

*I will try not to put others on pedestals.*
*It makes it too easy for them to fall off.*

*First—if you are in love—that's a good thing—*
*that's about the best thing that can happen to anyone.*
*—John Steinbeck*

Enjoy the phases of courtship. Get to know each other in different moods, different months. But don't rush to make affection official or to label it or to be physical.

Epictetus wrote, "Nothing great is created suddenly, any more than a bunch of grapes or a fig. I answer you that there must be time. Let it first blossom, then bear fruit, then ripen." Steinbeck also said of love, "The main thing is not to hurry."

Kissing means more when feelings and trust have had time to grow. If you kiss a boy you just met, he may act like a stranger the next day—and he may be one. If you kiss a boy you've been going out with for a long time (three days is not a long time), your relationship may evolve into something long-lasting and deeper—and may someday become a memory you will cherish. Or more!

"The remembrance of your love crept into my heart like spring quietly invading the wilderness . . ." wrote Faiz Ahmed Faiz, a Pakistani poet.

*I will wait until the time is right.*

*Love is like quicksilver in the hand. Leave the fingers
open and it stays. Clutch it and it darts away.*
—Dorothy Parker

❀

You like him. He likes you. Things are looking good. Should you meet him after every class? Announce that you're going out? Insist that he never smile at another girl?

Love, like a cat, resists being cornered. If you get possessive, he may want to bolt. And if you worry every time he talks to another girl, you may drive him and yourself crazy.

So what if he chats with other girls? Isn't his dynamic exuberance one of the qualities you like about him? So what if you talk to other guys? Isn't your friendly openness one of the qualities he admires in you? Do you really want to dampen each other's spirits?

St. Paul wrote in a letter to the Corinthians: "Love is patient, love is kind, love is not jealous."

Feeling jealous? The best way to fight "the green-eyed monster" (as Shakespeare called jealousy) is to have faith not just in your boyfriend but in yourself. Think of yourself as a great person who deserves a great boyfriend—not as an unworthy person who somehow got lucky.

**Love is not a mousetrap.**

*Say "I love you" to those you love.*

—*George Eliot*

❀

If you have a boyfriend, let him know you appreciate him. The more graciously you love, the more you are loved. Instead of taking love for granted, can you celebrate it? Can you exchange little presents, compliments, notes, e-mails, words? Can you reassure those you care about that you think of them often and fondly?

Be aware that "I love you" means different things to different people. "The word 'love' has by no means the same sense for both sexes, and this is one of the serious misunderstandings that divide them," wrote Simone de Beauvoir. There is no urgent need to say "I love you" to the boy you just started going out with. Wait longer and the words mean more. If it's really love, won't there be time for pronouncements? If it's not—if the relationship might be kaput by Friday—then all the more reason not to go on record with the *L* word.

Some boys say "I love you" too often. If he whispers he loves you even though you don't know each other well, try not to lose your bearings or feel pressured to repeat the words. You can tell him how much you care about him or show how happy you are with him. But say "I love you" only if you mean it.

*I will celebrate those I love.*

*Let there be spaces in your togetherness.*

—*Kahlil Gibran*

❀

Why smother each other? Why stick together like superglue? Why press redial the moment you hang up? Or IM him every single time he goes on-line? Give each other breathing room and you'll have more to talk about when you're hand in hand.

Pay attention to each other, yes, but keep doing what you did before he came along. See your girlfriends, do your homework, practice the trombone, surf the net. He, too, should stay involved with friends, schoolwork, extracurricular activities. You want to be adding to each other's lives, not taking away. And you want to continue growing as individuals, not pressing pause on your development.

Rainer Maria Rilke wrote: "Love consists in this, that two solitudes protect and border and greet each other."

Resist the urge to merge: One half plus one half equals only one.

Be individuals: One plus one equals two.

**My love life is not my whole life.**

*I am always a perfectly safe man to tell any dirt to,*
*as it goes in one ear and out my mouth.*

—*Ernest Hemingway*

❀

Be a keeper of secrets and people will open up to you. Be a blabbermouth and no one will tell you anything worth blabbing.

And when it's your secret? Your cool crush? Your hot date? If you don't want anyone to know, don't tell anyone. If you do want or need to discuss something, be candid with one trustworthy friend or confide in a friend or cousin in another town. There is no need to make your private life public or to forward your boyfriend's e-mailed love note to everyone on your buddy list.

If you do spill your news far and wide with a promise-not-to-tell tagline, your buddies may use your secret to spice up their e-mails and conversations. It's too much to hope that they can keep their mouths closed if you cannot.

As the Talmud puts it: "Thy friend has a friend, and thy friend's friend has a friend; be discreet." And as William Congreve wrote, "O fie miss, you must not kiss and tell."

*To kiss and tell is all very well,*
*but it's better to kiss and shut up.*

*We must develop and maintain the capacity to forgive.*
*He who is devoid of the power to forgive*
*is devoid of the power to love.*
—*Martin Luther King, Jr.*

❀

Your boyfriend was an hour late, and you're mad. Yet he's usually prompt. And he did apologize profusely. And it wasn't entirely his fault. And he understands why you're angry.

What should you do? Let him off the hook.

If you care about someone, is it worth it to stay mad or bear grudges? Rather than hold on to a hurt, express your disappointment, talk it over, and move on.

Love is not static. Once you have a boyfriend, it's not as though you put a big check by "Love" and that's that. Romances ebb and flow, wane and grow. As Ursula K. LeGuin wrote, "Love doesn't just sit there, like a stone. It has to be made, like bread, remade all the time, like new."

Love requires adjustments and fine tuning. If you're the one who caused him pain or did something wrong, don't be too proud to say you're sorry. Reconciliation can bring you closer than ever.

*I will not simmer in silence.*

*He that cheats me once, shame on him;*
*he that cheats me twice, shame on me.*
—*Scottish proverb*

❀

To err is human; to forgive, divine. But if you keep forgiving and forgiving and forgiving, he's a jerk and you're a chump.

Let's just say your steady boyfriend of several months kissed another girl while you were away on spring vacation. You would never have known except that her best friend told you. Now you're devastated. He confesses all, apologizes, and says he loves you and hopes you'll forgive him. Fine. You do. But what if you find out that he and that other girl went out again last Saturday, even though he told you he was going bowling with the guys? Now what?

Cut your losses. Don't blame her; blame him. Do you want a steady boyfriend who can't be trusted? There are billions of guys in this world. He is just one. It's better to lose a boyfriend than to lose your dignity.

So yank out Cupid's arrow and let the wound heal. You are not the only one who has been leveled by love. You know *The Scream* by Edvard Munch? He wrote, "I shall paint people who breathe and feel and suffer and love." Love can sometimes hurt—but it shouldn't *usually* hurt.

**Just because love is blind doesn't mean I am.**

*Almost every relationship I've ever been in*
*has basically been a train wreck.*

—*Ben Affleck*

❀

"Sometimes your heart will ache," sang Ma Rainey. Sometimes we sing the blues. If your calls are not returned, your e-mail box is empty, and he doesn't meet your eyes, take the hint. "No answer is also an answer," goes a German proverb.

Some boys are incapable of explaining why they feel the way they do. Some count on your reading between the lines and knowing that a romance is over—or will never begin.

While gentle explanations might be handy, they are rarely offered. Many loves end abruptly or never get started, and no words ease the pain or clear the confusion.

What about when a boy likes you and you don't like him? Do you always sit him down and tell him why? Probably not. You may just go about your business and hope he gets the message. Silence is easy and can save face. That's why girls and guys both need to strive to figure out what others are saying, even when they aren't using words, or the words aren't the ones you want to hear. (Pssst, boys have feelings, too. Justin Timberlake said, "I know one lesson I'm going to have to learn in this lifetime is how to let go.")

*If the writing is on the wall, I will read it.*

*Hearts will never be practical*
*until they are made unbreakable.*

——*L. Frank Baum*

❀

Beyoncé Knowles said, "We're not just these strong women with hearts made of stone that can never be cut."

Not every great boyfriend would make a great husband or a great father. Still, it hurts when love turns to ash. When you open yourself to the joy of love, you also open yourself to the pain of loss. And longing. Julia Glass writes of "the exhaustion of a longing so relentless it had become nearly unconscious, as if I had failed to realize that the water I drank was salty, always salty."

If you are newly alone, call your girlfriends—the ones you didn't drop the moment you had a boyfriend, remember? Invite them over for dinner or a slumber party. Tell them you're glad they are there and how much they mean to you. Let them lift your spirits.

Although this particular boyfriend is now history, you'll have chemistry with someone else soon. Someone you may never have known had you been tied up in a relationship.

**Girlfriends often last longer than boyfriends.**

*Love is so short and forgetting is so long.*

—*Pablo Neruda*

❀

Alfred, Lord Tennyson said the famous line: "'Tis better to have loved and lost than never to have loved at all." Be gentle with yourself. Don't bicycle past his home or play your song or cry for three days straight or press send on an e-mail when you should press delete. Instead, write a poem or get a new haircut or go to an art museum or catch up on your journal or organize your closet or read a novel. Focus on friends, family, schoolwork, yourself. Get as busy as you were before you loaned him your heart.

Falling out of love can be harder than falling in. Don't deny the sadness—it is a tribute to your ability to love—but don't become the sadness either. If it helps you to heal, remind yourself of the things that annoyed you about him and of the moments that weren't blissful.

You'll always remember your first love. Someday, you'll even be able to recall the happy times with fondness instead of tears. You were important chapters in each other's lives. But there are many chapters still ahead. The end of one thing is the beginning of something else.

**He was my first love—not my last love.**

*I have learned not to worry about love but*
*to honor its coming with all my heart.*
—*Alice Walker*

❀

With warm water and a day or two, you can force forsythia branches to burst into bloom. But you can't force someone to love you, and you can't love someone against your will.

So don't work so hard at it. Just continue to express yourself with sincerity and humor, and send out cheery e-mails or invitations to jump-start your social life. Be friendly and allow others to confide in you about their worries and disappointments and hopes. Allow them to be as real as you are.

When you least expect it, love will swing by again, in all its richness and complexity. As the Italians say, "Every hill has its valley." Lonely periods do end.

For now, maintain perspective. Did you lose your family in an earthquake? Do you have running water and food? How bleak are things really? "Learn to be happy," Anna Quindlen told graduates at a college commencement: Life can be "glorious, and you have no business taking it for granted."

*Behind passing clouds, the sun still shines.*

*A lady of forty-seven who has been married*
*twenty-seven years and has six children knows*
*what love really is and once described it for me like this:*
*"Love is what you've been through with somebody."*
———*James Thurber*

Many girls' mothers and fathers are no longer married. Many other girls listen to their parents argue and wonder, "Did they ever really love each other?" Chances are, they did—and still do. But adults suffer constant unromantic distractions, from paying bills and worrying about taxes to taking out the trash. Don't just roll your eyes at your parents' relationship. You may want to do things differently. But navigating the narrows together counts for something. And the day-to-day lifelong love married parents have is real, too—and in some ways harder to sustain than the love you and your friends enjoy on dates and at dances.

If your parents aren't together, you may feel extra-cautious about love (if you care about him, will he leave?). If your parents are constantly busy, whether they're married or divorced, you may feel extra hungry for love. Whatever your circumstance, try to find a balance of daring to love but protecting yourself, of being open but not being too vulnerable.

*Family love counts, too.*

# Family

*One of the oldest human needs is having someone*
*to wonder where you are when you*
*don't come home at night.*
—*Margaret Mead*

❦

Next time your mom or dad won't let you stay out late, ask yourself why they worry. Your parents look out for you because they love you. They're protective—possibly over-protective—out of concern for your safety.

You may think, "They don't trust me!" But is that really it? They may trust *you*, but not the world. And, sad but true, they may have a point. The world isn't always trustworthy. Most strangers are nice; some are dangerous. Which is all the more reason why it's lucky to have a family. Parents who care. A door to close. A safe haven.

Basketball superstar Shaquille O'Neal said, "I had older friends but they were knuckleheads, and you can't go to knuckleheads for life lessons. So when I needed guidance, I looked to my mother or my father."

**Families rule.**

*Happiness is having a large, loving, caring,*
*close-knit family in another city.*

—George Burns

❦

Do you sometimes feel that way? Or do you love your family as much as Jo in *Little Women*, who said, "I do think families are the most beautiful things in all the world!"?

When families get along, it's the best. Even when parents are too strict or busy or moody, it's good to know they're there. They can bail you out of a jam or pick you up if you get stranded. When you're sick, it's a parent, not a buddy, who helps in the middle of the night and serves up chicken soup the next day. And though siblings squabble, blood is thicker than water, and most siblings stick up for each other when necessary.

Do you treat your parents and siblings as though you're the sun and they're distant planets? Do they treat you the same way? What would happen if you treated them with respect and appreciation? It might set a better tone for everybody.

*My family is not perfect, but neither am I.*

*You have to leave your nest in order to fly.*

—*Carlos Santana*

❀

Most parents try to give kids roots and wings, and most also have concerns of their own. Even when your parents are testing you on spelling words, or reminding your kid brother to flush the toilet or your big sister about SATs, they may be worried about bills, termites, health, their marriage, or their parents.

If you want to be heard, it helps to listen. Can you ask your parents about their day at home or at work? When your parents come home from a business trip, can you ask, "How'd it go?" instead of "What did you bring me?" Think about what (besides you) might be on their minds and show interest. Consider saying, "I miss you" rather than complaining, "You're always busy." That will warm them up rather than put them on the defensive. The trick is to try to be a caring daughter and a daring person . . . to make peace with your parents so you can move forward.

Twelve years after Paul McCartney's mother died, the Beatle had a dream. "My mother appeared . . . and she said to me very gently, very reassuringly, 'Let it be.'"

*I know where I come from;*
*I'm learning where I want to go.*

*The greatest love is a mother's; then comes a dog's;*
*then a sweetheart's.*
—*Polish proverb*

❀

Boyfriends come and go. Moms stick around. Pearl S. Buck wrote, "Some are kissing mothers and some are scolding mothers, but it is love just the same, and most mothers kiss and scold together."

It's true that most mothers want your dress to cover your thighs. And don't want you to dye your hair green. Or pierce your navel. Or get tattoos. But just as you'd like to get along with your mom, she'd like to get along with you. Which means you have the same goal. Can you work on it? Can you find a moment between breakfast chaos and bedtime scramble to talk about what has made either of you proud—or upset? If you've had a fight, can you make up? Can you say, "I disagree," instead of "You're wrong," or even "I see your point," instead of insisting on the last word? Can you compliment your mom on her hair, dinner, work? Can you call or e-mail or leave a note in her purse or under her pillow? If you behave toward her, for one minute, as warmly as you do toward your best friend's mom, you'll both come out ahead.

**Nobody's mother gets it right all the time.**

*I always thought when I was young that my mother was wrong. You eventually come to the realization that she was correct about everything.*

—*Reese Witherspoon*

❀

Parents aren't always right or always wrong.

Are you and your mom incredibly close? So close that you don't want to go to slumber parties, sleepaway camp, or your aunt's for the weekend? Uh-oh. If you're too dependent, it may be time to try to walk out of her shadow.

Or are you and your mom at odds? Yesterday you loved it when she bought you dresses and held your hand. Today you hate her fashion taste and you'd never touch her hand. Uh-oh. If you're forging your own identity so effectively that Mom's left in the dust, remember that she is not evil incarnate and that you can separate without disconnecting.

Lance Armstrong wrote, "My mom is one of the most influential people in my life, if not *the* most. She wasn't an athlete like me, but she was a good lady, a strong lady."

**My mother loves me in her way.**

*When I was a boy of fourteen,*
*my father was so ignorant, I could hardly stand*
*to have the old man around. But when I got to be*
*twenty-one, I was astonished at how much*
*the old man had learned in seven years.*

—*Mark Twain*

❀

Are you mad at your dad? Did you announce that you were going to take a spin on Spike's motorcycle—and Dad blew a gasket? Chances are your father is not out to make your life miserable. Chances are he wants the best for you.

Hillary Rodham Clinton said, "My parents set really high expectations for me and were rarely satisfied. I would come home from school with a good grade and my father would say, 'It must have been an easy assignment.'" Infuriating? Yes. But he meant it to be motivating—and perhaps it was.

Is your dad too tough? Too quick to anger? Too committed to his work? Or to a stepfamily? Colette says, "It is not a bad thing that children should occasionally, and politely, put parents in their place." Yet years down the road, you may reassess your old man. You may even decide that he did the best he could. Goethe wrote, "Life teaches us to be less severe with ourselves and others."

**Growing up includes growing pains.**

*We've had bad luck with our kids—they've all grown up.*

—Christopher Morley

❀

If you and your parent love each other, you're both blessed. If you can talk and laugh and play cards and run errands and see movies and share pistachio nuts, you are both extraordinarily lucky. Go wild. Leave a note in your parents' briefcase or jacket pocket. Or add zing to their voice mail or e-mail. Or just give them an extra smile and hug. Ideally, your parents are proud of who you are. Not just your class election or good grades or goal in soccer or role in the play, but who *you* are.

Bill Clinton gave a speech at his daughter Chelsea's high school graduation and said, "I ask you . . . to indulge your folks if we seem a little sad or we act a little weird . . . a part of us longs to hold you once more as we did when you could barely walk, and to read to you just one more time *Goodnight Moon*."

In *The Secret Life of Bees*, the narrator realizes, "No matter how much you thought you could leave your mother behind, she would never disappear from the tender places in you."

**If I love my parents, I can say so.**

*The best advice anyone ever gave me came from my dad:*
*Do it right the first time or don't do it at all.*
—*Ashton Kutcher*

❁

Maybe your father gives great advice. But what if he doesn't? What if yours tends to be mean or grumpy or absent or drunk?

That's harsh. But many kids have complicated home lives.

If your father is always disapproving and refuses to get help, there may come a point when you will need to stop looking to him for approval. If you continue to seek reassurance from a distant or abusive parent who just can't give it, you'll feel worse. Better to look elsewhere for guidance and support. Yes, this is a shame for you and a loss for your parent. While he's yelling (or just plain gone), he's shutting himself off from a bond that could have been wonderful. (Publilius Syrus said, "An angry father is most cruel toward himself.") Someday a mentor may take a fatherly interest in you. And someday if you have kids of your own, you can be there for them. Who knows? In the future, you and your parent may even manage an adult-to-adult relationship after all.

*I can bloom even in thin soil.*

*Much unhappiness has come into the world because of bewilderment and things left unsaid.*
—Fyodor Dostoyevsky

❀

You think your mom has been acting weird or mean or distracted because of your school conference. But it's really because she's worried about layoffs at work. She thinks you're acting sullen because you're mad at her. But actually you're mad at your best friend for flirting with your boyfriend.

Can you try harder to fill in the blanks for each other? If your parents are trying to talk about something that makes you uncomfortable, make an effort to hear them out. And if you want to broach an awkward subject, consider doing so over dishes, cards, in a car, on the phone, or even on-line. Heart-to-hearts are sometimes easiest when you're not face-to-face.

Some girls complain that their parents invade their privacy. No one should read your diary or listen in on your calls. But don't be so secretive that you leave your parents in the dark. If they ask, "Where are you going?" and you mumble, "Out," that won't lead to deeper trust and closer communication. And parents do need to know what you're up to. It's one of the requirements of their job.

*I won't shut out my parents.*

*Parents are not quite interested in justice,*

*they are interested in quiet.*

—*Bill Cosby*

❀

Some parents struggle to help children resolve conflicts; some accidentally pit kids against one another; and some just wish kids would work things out on their own.

If your parents have given you negotiating skills and a healthy respect for one another, you're ahead of the game. If, instead, they label you ("the pretty one," "the brain," "the soccer star," "the little one") or prod you to compete ("On your mark, get set, go! Winner gets a treat!"), that's less ideal.

Try to think of siblings as teammates, not rivals. You will be important to each other all your lives, so you might as well make peace—for your sake and your parents'. Can you praise each other instead of cut each other down? Can you seek different activities instead of signing up together for ballet, band, or baseball? Try this: treat your siblings, for three minutes, with the same courtesy you reserve for friends and see how they respond. You can't break up with your family, but you can break old patterns. As Nelson Mandela said, "The moment to bridge the chasms that divide us has come."

**I can call the truce.**

*The highlight of my childhood was making my brother*
*laugh so hard that food came out of his nose.*

—*Garrison Keillor*

❁

Aristotle said, "Cruel is the strife of brothers." Do you make your siblings laugh—or cry?

Too many families are rife with fraternal friction. If you and your brother constantly snarl, snap, bite, and fight, remind yourself that you are not lion cubs picking over a dead wildebeest. You're humans. You can do better.

Next time your brother taunts you, don't tell on him—talk to him. Say you're sorry you two don't get along better. Compliment something, anything. ("That poster looks great on your wall." "You're so good at ————.") Instead of bickering, offer popcorn or homework help, or ask his advice, or talk about a relative. Get a decent relationship going—it's not impossible. As Mother Teresa said, "Kind words can be short and easy to speak, but their echoes are truly endless."

If you are the one who picks fights, try to change that. If he starts them, say, "I don't want to argue." And if you always ban your kid brother from your room, invite him in for a quick game of cards or Clue or Sorry. It may make his day.

**When siblings fight, nobody wins.**

*I wanted to be Venus. I did everything Venus did.*

—*Serena Williams*

❀

Some sisters get along famously. Some fight like cats. The most fortunate sisters become friends for life.

Are you in the shadow of a super sister? Work on your own strong suits. Does your big sister boss you around? Stick up for yourself without shouting or pouting. Do you have a crush on her boyfriend? Don't even think about acting on it. Is your sister away at camp or school? Write or send a care package. "Big sisters are the crabgrass in the lawn of life," said Charles Schulz, who created *Peanuts*.

Are you the big sister? You can be teacher, friend, ally. Encourage your kid sister, in school and out. Ask how a test or audition went. Do chores or errands together. Recognize that she has some strengths you don't. And share—you'll both reap benefits.

Will you two get along every minute? No. But as Mahatma Gandhi said, "It is possible to live in peace." Learning how to befriend, not belittle, siblings also teaches you to compromise, cooperate, and be comfortable with people outside your family.

If you have siblings, can you name something you admire about them?

**I can be civil to my siblings.**

*Live so that you wouldn't be ashamed*
*to sell the family parrot to the town gossip.*

—*Will Rogers*

❁

"I wish you were never born!" "I hate your guts!" "You are such an idiot!" "You are the stupidest person in the world."

Siblings get crazy-mad because they love each other. You'd never shriek at someone you just met. You'd never say you hate the school nurse. But when you really care about someone, and you feel safe enough to express your rage, fights can get fierce. Why? Because deep down you believe that your relationship can survive. Henry David Thoreau said, "Those whom we can love, we can hate; to others we are indifferent."

Accept the range of emotions that is part of family life. Anger, like a summer thunderstorm, comes and goes. But temper your temper. Don't fire the first shot or insist on firing the last.

**When people care, passions flare.**

*There is no such thing as fun for the whole family.*

*—Jerry Seinfield*

❀

This is almost true, especially if your family includes both toddlers and teens. But instead of slamming your bedroom door, blasting your music, and being mad that your family never does fun things together, think about how you (yes, you) can come up with a creative solution.

The whole family might enjoy renting a classic movie, like *The Wizard of Oz*. Or going out for pizza or ice cream or a walk. Or making bread or soup or sugar cookies. Or playing hearts or charades or Monopoly. Or spending a day at a beach, or mountain.

Start your own traditions. Saturday afternoon at the movies. Sunday morning pancakes. A once-a-week after-dinner reading—everyone reads a poem or a passage from a book aloud. Different ages, different choices, but no teasing, because the point is family closeness.

*I can help make a day memorable.*

*Remember that as a teenager you are*
*at the last stage in your life when you will be*
*happy to hear that the phone is for you.*

—Fran Lebowitz

✿

Want to reach out and touch someone? Some families fall apart because of the phone. Everyone wants to hog it. Or messages get mangled. Or no one respects call waiting and crucial calls never get through.

Set ground rules. During that rare event known as Family Dinner, it's a shame if Dad's on the horn to the office or you're on your cell discussing homework. Why not agree to screen calls during meals? If the phone rings, it's probably not your heartthrob, sigh, but some stranger asking for a donation. You can also discuss time limits (no calls after ten?) and whether a cell phone, separate line, e-mail, answering machine, or caller I.D. might help.

When you are on the phone, remember not to interrupt or yak endlessly. Fran Lebowitz quipped, "The opposite of talking isn't listening. The opposite of talking is waiting." It's okay to be chatty. But if someone called you, find out why.

**I will play fair with the phone.**

*Divorce is probably of nearly the same date as marriage.*
*I believe, however, that marriage is some weeks*
*the more ancient.*

—*Voltaire*

❀

Many siblings fight one moment and are friends the next. Many parents argue, then make up. Yet for some parents, there is no reconciliation.

If your parents get divorced, the adjustment is painful and sad and slow. Who else in your class has parents who are divorced? In America, nearly one out of three kids lives with a single parent. Don't bottle up feelings. Talk with friends about denial, anger, guilt, hurt, shock, relief. If you keep wishing your parents would reconnect, be realistic and briefly remember the worst fights. Remind yourself, too, that the divorce was not your fault: Your parents divorced each other—not you. And as Margaret Trudeau said, "It takes two to destroy a marriage."

Try to appreciate both your parents, rather than take sides. If one parent gets you through homework and the other provides fun, fun, fun, both are trying to care for you. If one parent shuttles you from orthodontist to piano lesson, and the other sends gifts or cards, both are showing love. And if only one parent is there for you, that hurts, but the love of one parent can see you through.

*I still have a family.*

*There are fathers who do not love their children;*
*there is no grandfather who does not*
*adore his grandson.*

—*Victor Hugo*

❦

While some grandparents are more involved than others, most show off your photos, are eager for your news, and can't wait until your visits. Are your grandparents alive and well? Do you take them for granted?

Call, fax, and write letters. Send drawings, photos, e-mail, good report cards. Consider confiding in them. Grandparents have seen a lot and may have good advice. Many also have good stories—about the olden days and your own parent's misdeeds and exploits. What were your grandparents like at your age? What was your parent like as a kid? Ask.

Do your grandparents give you birthday or holiday presents? Do you blow off writing them thank-you notes? How would you feel if you sent someone a gift and never even heard if it got there? As for gift giving, sure, you can just sign your name on your parents' gift card. But why not make something yourself? Homemade stuff goes over big—whether it's edible, wearable, or ideal for displaying on the refrigerator or coffee table.

**I will appreciate my grandparents.**

*If you wish to succeed, consult three old people.*

—*Chinese proverb*

❀

Some kids and teenagers dismiss their wrinkled relatives as a bunch of old fogies. Mistake. Older people have been around for decades and will share stories and insights free of charge. Wisdom doesn't automatically come with age, yet many experienced adults are able to see situations clearly.

When your aunt or great-aunt offers advice on what to do about your teacher or boyfriend or neighbor, you don't have to heed it. But it doesn't hurt to hear her opinion.

Above all, don't act like you've been-there-done-that. Writer Mavis Gallant described a respectful man who "never once remarked, 'I've heard this before,' or uttered the time-less, frantic snub of the young, 'I know, I know, *I know*.'" Why not go ahead and show some respect? Your older relatives will be flattered by the attention—even if you ultimately choose to take their advice with heaps of salt.

**Aunts and uncles are there when I need them.**

*The problem with death is that it lasts forever.*

—*Gabriel García Márquez*

❀

When a member of your family dies, you may feel that a part of you has died, too. Be gentle with yourself. Don't expect to feel better in a hurry. But don't deny yourself the right to ever laugh or feel good again. Share your sorrow with parents and siblings who may also be grieving. And, if possible, remember the loved one on paper: in a poem or sketch or melody or work of art.

May Sarton asked, "What is there to do when people die—people so dear and rare—but bring them back by remembering?" Someday, in months or years, you'll be able to remember the good times with fondness instead of sorrow. You may also become stronger and more compassionate than you ever were before. You won't moan, "This is the worst day of my life" when you misplace your homework. You'll be able to distinguish little troubles from big ones. You'll be able to comfort others in their moment of need, and you'll know that you have a well of strength and resilience. Wrote Dylan Thomas: "After the first death, there is no other."

*A person who is dead can be alive and*
*safe in my memory.*

*The sorrow for the dead is the only sorrow from which we refuse to be divorced. Every other wound we seek to heal, every other affliction to forget; but this wound we consider it a duty to keep open; this affliction we cherish and brood over in solitude.*

—*Washington Irving*

❀

Of course we do. That's how much we loved the person who is gone, whether he or she is absent because of death or divorce. Death and divorce are extremely hard to accept. But as architect Maya Lin said, "Only when you accept the pain can you come away from it."

If months and months go by and you don't feel one bit better, give yourself permission to start bouncing back. It is not a betrayal of a dead or absent father to laugh or to smile at a mother's new boyfriend. It is not a betrayal of a missing mom to joke and be silly with friends or to befriend your father's girlfriend.

No one would want you to grieve forever. Talk to a doctor or counselor if you find yourself tangled up in memories or anger. Then, without rushing things, invite yourself to enjoy life again.

*I can be like a trick birthday candle:*
*I can make a comeback.*

*Honor thy father and thy mother.*
—*Exodus 20:12*

❀

It makes sense to honor your parents. But some kids don't live with their parents. Some have parents who aren't honorable. And some never knew their birth parents but love and honor their adoptive parents who chose to love and raise them. (They *are* their parents.)

An African proverb says, "It takes a village to raise a child." Gloria Steinem once wrote: "The biological family isn't the only important unit in society; we have needs and longings that our families cannot meet."

If your parent or parents can't always be there for you, reach out to other trusted adults. You may find a mentor or role model in your aunt, teacher, coach, minister, priest, or rabbi. If you're an only child, enjoy the fact that your room is quiet, but look to cousins, neighbors, and friends. Find people who care about you and who matter to you—family or not.

**Sharing love can be as important as sharing genes.**

*The great pleasure of a dog is that you may make a fool of yourself with him and not only will he not scold you, he will make a fool of himself too.*

—*Samuel Butler*

❁

As Charles Schulz put it, "Happiness is a warm puppy." Dogs are family members, too. So are cats. And bunnies, guinea pigs, turtles, snakes, fish, frogs, hamsters, gerbils, mice, rats, iguanas, lizards, and birds of all sorts—even horses, if you're lucky. What am I overlooking here? A treasured ant farm? Beetles in a bug box? A pot-bellied pig? A cow?

After enduring much criticism, President Harry Truman once remarked, "If you want a friend in Washington, get a dog." Dogs and other pets are faithful when others let you down. They love you even on bad days and even when you want to be alone—but not totally alone.

Are you taking good care of your pet? Do you feed it on schedule? Keep its home clean? Show it affection? You can let your parents do all the work. But why not take on the job yourself? Tail wagging and purring will be your rewards. And you'll find satisfaction in feeling needed and doing an important job well.

**My pet and I are lucky to have each other.**

# School

*We don't need no education—*
*We don't need no thought control—*
*——Pink Floyd*

❀

Then again, William Butler Yeats put it this way: "Education is not the filling of a pail, but the lighting of a fire." School isn't just about making the grade and getting the diploma. It's about learning to learn and learning to love learning. About liking the novel you read in English so much that you search for another book by the same author. About enjoying Spanish class so much that you attempt conversation with someone who speaks only Spanish. About relishing how good it feels to solve a hard math problem. About botching the experiment in science, doing it over, getting it right, and realizing that failure can lead to success. About finding friends who make you laugh and friends who make you think. School can teach you how to keep your brain awake after classes, too. To observe, read, think, grow, learn. School can teach you to be a student of the world.

"Anyone who stops learning is old, whether at twenty or eighty," said Henry Ford. "Anyone who keeps learning stays young."

*Others may sleepwalk, but I am awake.*

*I was raised to think and to question.*

—*Nicole Kidman*

Maria Montessori said, "Education must start from birth." When you were a wide-eyed baby, a reckless toddler, and an adventurous kindergartner, you were learning, learning, learning. Using your brain and five senses, you were processing information faster than a computer. And you still are. As Carl Sandburg pointed out, "Time is a great teacher."

By now you know why ambulances have sirens and why you shouldn't pet a strange dog without asking its owner. You have knowledge. You have experience.

But you're not done. Madeleine L'Engle, author of *A Wrinkle in Time*, said, "I do not think I will ever reach a stage when I will say, 'This is what I believe. Finished.' What I believe is alive and open to growth." Keep your eyes and ears and mind open—even when you're walking down the same path or listening to the same teacher or dining with the same relative. If you approach the familiar in a fresh way, you'll keep learning. In school and out.

**Questions are as important as answers.**

*People are stupid,*
*and I say that with the greatest respect.*
—*Jackie Mason*

❀

Lois Wyse said, "Men are taught to apologize for their weaknesses, women for their strength." Be as smart and as strong as you can be.

Run with your talents. Live up to your potential. Be proud of your gifts. You're a great student? Raise your hand. Your butterfly stroke is awesome? Go for the gold. You draw lifelike portraits? Keep a sketch pad in your backpack.

If your prowess intimidates others, whose problem is that? Don't act superior. Just be superior. But also be considerate and confident and a good sport, not a competitive win-or-whine know-it-all. If you happen to be smart/athletic/artistic/stunning, enjoy the cards you were dealt and let others enjoy them, too. Friends won't be put off by your strengths unless you start getting an attitude or acting falsely modest. Which you won't, right?

Are you worried that a certain guy won't like you if you're better at tennis or math than he is? Excuse me? He'd prefer a klutz or a ditz? Let him find one instead of slowing you down. Be your best and you will attract guys who are inspired by excellence—not afraid of it.

**I will never play dumb.**

*Ideas come from everywhere.*

—*Alfred Hitchcock*

❀

The teacher says, "Write a poem." You think, "I don't know what to write."

Think again.

Write about the way shadows stretch. The way jeans fade. The way geese fly. The way you-know-who smiles. Write about Buddha or Bach or the Beatles. Write about a quote in this book.

Anna Quindlen wrote, "People have writer's block not because they can't write, but because they despair of writing eloquently." Just put pen to paper—or fingers to keyboard. Later you can revise and improve your work. As Jacques Barzun wrote, "You are working on paper, not eternal bronze. Let that first sentence be as stupid as it wishes."

You can make your way through the fog. Don't say, "I don't know," say, "Let me think." Take yourself seriously.

And find a teacher who believes in you. "A little spark of belief goes a long way," said Sarah Jessica Parker.

**I won't get stuck.**

*The thousand-mile journey starts with one step.*

*—Japanese proverb*

❀

Sometimes a teacher asks for a term paper, and the task starts to loom larger and larger in your mind until it seems all but impossible. You feel defeated, panicked, unable to begin.

What to do?

Begin. Stop thinking of it as scaling Mount Everest. Think of it as going for a walk, uphill perhaps, and take it step by step. Books like this begin with single quotes. Reports like yours begin with taking notes. Break your work into manageable chunks, push up your sleeves, and dig in, bit by bit by bit.

Even presidents and kings have to chip away at huge projects before feeling the satisfaction of completion. Said Calvin Coolidge: "We cannot do everything at once, but we can do something at once." Said England's Albert I: "The first reward of a work accomplished is having done it."

And even Sir Edmund Hillary, who *did* climb Mount Everest with Tenzing Norgay, said, "You don't have to be a fantastic hero to do certain things. . . . you can be just an ordinary chap, sufficiently motivated." Chap—or lass!

*I won't get overwhelmed; I'll get started.*

*Procrastination is the art of keeping up with yesterday.*

—Don Marquis

✿

It's smart to work methodically and to accomplish your goals in a slow-and-steady way instead of a stop-and-start way. After all, what if something trips you up? Something bad, like falling on your chin and needing stitches? Or something good, like being invited by your crush to a concert on Thursday when your report is due on Friday?

The work is not going to go away, so get it done. Mark Twain quipped, "Never put off until tomorrow what you can put off till the day after tomorrow." Ben Franklin said it straight: "One today is worth two tomorrows."

Once you start, it's easier to keep going. So stay organized. Keep lists of top-priority projects and daily assignments. Clear away clutter. Imagine how good it will feel when you finish.

*If I don't fall behind, I'll come out ahead.*

*I arise in the morning torn between a desire to improve*
*(or save) the world and a desire to enjoy (or savor)*
*the world. This makes it hard to plan the day.*

—*E. B. White*

❀

Do you plan your day? Are you aware of how you spend your time? "An inch of gold cannot purchase an inch of time," goes a Chinese saying.

Some people fritter away their days and fail to get their work done. Others stick to a ruthless schedule and forget to have any fun. It's a challenge to meet goals and to meet friends, to work and to work out, to get enough rest and to sleep. But you can decide what to do with your time.

Many people say, "I don't have time to exercise," or "I don't have time to read for pleasure," or "I don't have time to practice piano." Yet everybody's day has the same twenty-four hours. Nobody gets more; nobody gets fewer. If something is important to you, don't wait until you have the time. Find the time. Make the time.

*I won't take chances; I'll make choices.*

*The difference between the right word*
*and the almost right word is the difference between*
*lightning and the lightning bug.*
—*Mark Twain*

❀

Your favorite aunt says, "So, how's school?" You say, "Fine. My friends are nice and we're studying interesting things." That's a whole lot better than grunting, but what have you really told your aunt? Not much.

Yes, your friend is nice. But is she also funny or graceful or shy or bilingual or generous or anxious or jealous or horse crazy or boy crazy? Yes, your class is interesting. But why not say you cried when you finished reading *Of Mice and Men*? Or that you learned why port cities like New York and New Orleans developed faster than inland cities. Give others something to talk to you about. Speak (and write) with precision. Search for the right word—*le môt juste*—instead of peppering your sentences with "you know" or "like" or lazy words or curse words. The more articulate and specific and eloquent you are, the more people will want to hear what you have to say. And the more succinctly you speak, the better. "Brevity is the soul of wit," as Shakespeare's Polonius put it—after rambling on and on.

*I won't strain for big words.*
*I will say what I mean.*

*The struggle is what teaches you.*

—Sue Grafton

❀

It's fun to be good at something. To be a whiz at math, a natural at science, the first one picked in gym.

Coasting along and doing what comes easily is fine. But if you never screw up, you may not be challenging yourself. Have you ever really put time and effort into a painting or speech or project or sport? Have you ever stuck with something until you succeeded—and felt proud? Confidence and expertise come after practice and patience.

You may feel you have reached a plateau. You're okay at swimming but you'll never be great. You're proficient at Italian, but you'll never be fluent. Can you keep going? Immerse yourself in the water—or the subjunctive. Find a coach or a teacher who can challenge you and advise you. If you don't give up, you can reach your goals. Euclid said, "There is no royal road to geometry." Venus Williams said, "So what if you fail? At least you'll know what *not* to do when you try again." Lisa Kudrow put it this way: "I've learned that you can make a mistake, and the world doesn't end."

**Opening night comes only after days of rehearsal.**

*Have you learned lessons only of those who admired you,*
*and were tender to you, and stood aside for you?*
*Have you not learned great lessons from*
*those who reject you . . . ?*
—*Walt Whitman*

❧

Sooner or later everyone gets a teacher she does not like—or who seems not to like her. Last year's teacher would have given you an A. This year's teacher tells you to work harder or doesn't "get" you. You probably badmouth her under your breath. But you may also stretch for a higher level of achievement—whether to make her proud or to prove her wrong.

Of course, this year's tough teacher may not be a stimulating fireball but a drone who doesn't recognize a good student when she's staring at one. This happens. In real life as well, there are tiresome landlords, unfair employers, cloying colleagues. If what you wind up learning from a tough teacher isn't how to study harder, but how to make the best of a less than ideal situation, that counts, too. Besides, as Anna Freud put it, "Creative minds have always been known to survive any kind of bad training." And as J. D. Salinger's Holden Caulfield pointed out, "You can't stop a teacher when they want to do something. They just *do* it."

*If I want to make waves,*
*I can't always expect smooth sailing.*

*You never hear any hints dropped on campus that*
*wisdom is supposed to be the goal of knowledge.*
—J. D. Salinger

❀

Goethe said, "They teach in academics far too many things and far too much that is useless." It can certainly feel that way. But you don't always know at age twelve or sixteen what you'll find useful (or essential) at age twenty or sixty. Today you may think, "Who cares about the conditional tense in French?" Then—voilà!—as an adult you might get transferred to Paris. Some lessons simply teach you to think, to question. Miguel de Unamuno wrote, "True science teaches, above all, to doubt and be ignorant."

School also exposes you to what's out there. T. S. Eliot wrote, "It is part of education to interest ourselves in subjects for which we have no aptitude." It's worth it to become a well-rounded person who can hold her own in any conversation and who can make a living in a satisfying way.

*I keep getting smarter—and wiser.*

*My alma mater was books . . . I could spend the rest of my life reading, just satisfying my curiosity.*

— Malcolm X

*The reading of all good books is like conversation with the finest minds of past centuries.*

— René Descartes

*A book is like a garden carried in the pocket.*

— Chinese proverb

*One of the greatest pleasures in my life is to be reading a really good book . . . and to know that after that one will be another really, really good book, and another . . . and another.*

— Oprah Winfrey

*I have never known any distress that an hour of reading did not relieve.*

— Montesquieu

*Books are . . . funny little portable pieces of thought.*

— Susan Sontag

A book must be an ice ax to break
the frozen sea within us.
—Franz Kafka


Books, books, books.
It was not that I read so much. I read and read
the same ones. But all of them were necessary to me.
Their presence, their smell, the letters of their titles,
and the texture of their leather bindings.
—Colette


It's not enough for me to read a book.
I have to "own" it. I scribble in the margins. . . .
I draw stars and exclamation points. . . .
—Twyla Tharp


Books are dangerous.
they make you think . . . feel . . . wonder. . . .
—Ray Bradbury


Read in order to live.
—Gustave Flaubert


Books are friends.
(Thanks for having this one in your hands.)

*It's never too late—in fiction or in life—to revise.*

—*Nancy Thayer*

❦

Next time you finish an essay, congratulate yourself for having done the hard part, but don't rush to hand it in early. Before bed, or perhaps the next day or week, reread your work and make it even better.

Cross out repetitive words or sentences. Delete awkward phrases or stilted words like *thus* or *hence*. Check your spelling. Give the beginning and ending more oomph. Read your work aloud to see if it's clear and to the point.

Most writers are rewriters. Said Vladimir Nabokov: "I have rewritten—often several times—every word I have ever published. My pencils outlast their erasers." Even if your words are not meant for publication, they are meant to be read. If you plan to sign your name to a report—or e-mail or love letter or thank-you note—have enough self-respect to edit, proofread, and fact-check your work. As Daniel Patrick Moynihan said, "Everyone is entitled to his own opinion, but not his own facts." And if you need to start something over, do so. "The wastepaper basket is a writer's best friend," said Isaac Bashevis Singer, Nobel laureate.

*I will reread my words before they leave my desk.*

*Every child is an artist. The problem is how
to remain an artist once he grows up.*

—*Pablo Picasso*

❀

Said Georgia O'Keeffe, "My painting is what I have to give back to the world for what the world gives to me." If you love to draw or paint or dance, you don't have to stop just because you're out of grade school. Your teachers may no longer expect illustrated book reports, but that doesn't mean you can't keep sketching on your own or spending Saturdays at museums and galleries. Nurture the artist within yourself. It's hard to make a living as a dancer, but if you can't live without dance, why not give it a try? At least keep attending classes and performances.

Why abandon artistic pursuits and pleasures just because you're devoting time to other subjects? Your aesthetic talents can be useful in many fields (book design, graphic art, landscaping, interior decorating). And your room and future office will always have flair. Besides, as sculptor Andy Goldsworthy said, "Good art keeps you warm."

Being efficient counts, but so does being expressive. Albert Einstein wrote, "Imagination is more important than knowledge." The byway can lead to places the highway does not.

*I will take care of the artist inside me.*

*Everyone has a talent. What is rare is the courage*
*to follow the talent to the dark places where it leads.*

—Erica Jong

❀

Art requires bravery and commitment. Artists sometimes need to be selfish, yet it's generous to share your gift and your vision.

Maybe the dark place where your talent leads is a dark room because you're a budding photographer. Develop your prints, your eye, and your discipline, and see if you can become the next Margaret Bourke-White or Diane Arbus or Annie Leibovitz. Maybe the dark place where your talent leads is a desk where you will write in silence and solitude while classmates are outside cheerleading or shooting hoops. If you want to write, love to write, *have* to write, then write. Maybe the dark place where your talent leads is the stage— before the curtain goes up and the lights go on. If you want to dance and act and sing, now is the time to work on your skills.

"Talent is like electricity," Maya Angelou once said. "We don't understand electricity. We use it."

You don't yet know what your talents are? That's okay. Keep reaching, branching out. Be ready to recognize your strong suits and chase your dreams.

*I will forgive myself if I fail,*
*but I won't forgive myself if I don't try.*

*This thing we call "failure" is not the falling down,*
*but the staying down.*
*—Mary Pickford*

❁

Miles Davis said, "Do not fear mistakes—there are none." Some teachers think Davis was mistaken. Was he? Instead of fearing mistakes, learn from them. Do you always play it safe? If you take no risks, you play no riffs. Or as Sophia Loren put it, "Mistakes are part of the dues one pays for living a full life."

No one is good at everything. Maybe your spelling is weak, yet your vocabulary is vast. Or maybe geometry is hard for you, yet you have more literary insights than your geometry teacher ever will. As Will Rogers wrote, "Everybody is ignorant, only on different subjects." Instead of being wowed or cowed by others, or self-conscious because you once repeated a year or did summer school, celebrate your strengths and work on what you need to work on. Even if you failed a course, that doesn't make *you* a failure. Move up a row in class, use spell check and dictionaries, take notes and review them, proofread your work, keep assignment pads, ask for a tutor, persevere. You can excel in the course you're best at, and you can improve in the one you find most difficult.

*I can be a good student*
*even if I'm not the best student.*

*I would prefer even to fail with honor*
*than to win by cheating.*

—*Sophocles*

❀

The problem with cheating is that sooner or later you get caught. If you plagiarize a paper from the Internet, a teacher may find out and flunk or expel you. Or you may get away with copying a friend's work, only to discover that French or math gets harder and harder. If you can't conjugate *avoir*, you can't do the *passé composé*. If you never learn multiplication, you will trip over simple equations all through school—and life. Try to stay on top of your lessons. Don't panic, prepare.

What if someone is out to copy your work? You don't need to report cheaters, but you don't need to help them either (especially when they are so good at helping themselves). You can cover your answers discreetly with your hand or arm or paper. Be proud of yourself for realizing that you are in school to learn, not to pretend to be learning. And be proud that you are not compromising your self-respect—which is something cheaters cannot crib. Said Aristotle: "Dignity does not consist in possessing honors, but in deserving them."

*Knowing I can do it beats hoping I can copy it.*

*I'm not one to brag, but I just might be*
*the smartest person who ever lived.*
—Conan O'Brien

❀

For some students, school is a piece of cake. For others, it's a steep climb. If your grades don't reflect your effort or intelligence, ask your parents or a guidance counselor what you can do. You may need to improve your organizational skills. You may need tutoring or summer classes. Or you may have a learning issue. If you have dyslexia or Attention Deficit Disorder, a medication or a new approach to learning may make all the difference. Helen Keller, who was blind, deaf, and confident, said, "I thank God for my handicaps, for, through them, I have found myself, my work, and my God."

What if it's not you but a friend or a family member who has trouble learning? Be understanding. Never tease anyone for her differences. Danny Glover was dyslexic and said, "Kids made fun of me. . . . Even as an actor, it took me a long time to realize why words and letters got jumbled up in my mind."

**Disabilities are a given. Insensitivity is a choice.**

*Every time I feel broke, I write a check to someone else.*

—*Caroline Rhea*

❀

How do *you* give back? "Service is the rent that you pay for room on this earth," said Shirley Chisholm.

People volunteer for all sorts of reasons. To have fun. To make friends. To help others. To improve skills. To show colleges that they have a good heart to go along with those good grades.

Are you interested in a cause that isn't offered in your school? Collecting coats for the homeless, or tutoring disadvantaged kids, or teaching English as a second language? "Human history," wrote Julio Cortázar, "is the sad result of each one looking out for himself."

You can look out for others by starting a community service, whether it's playing music at a residence for the elderly, or wrapping sandwiches at a soup kitchen.

"After all, what's a life, anyway?" asks Charlotte, E. B. White's altruistic arachnid. "We're born, we live a little while, we die . . . By helping you, perhaps I was trying to lift up my life a trifle. Heaven knows everyone's life can stand a little of that."

**Helping you helps me, too.**

*Kids always called me names, nasty names like*
*Shaquilla the Gorilla. When I started playing basketball,*
*everything changed. They were able to admire me instead*
*of laugh at me. Basketball saved my life.*

—*Shaquille O'Neal*

❀

Have you found a physical activity—basketball, soccer, track, gymnastics, yoga, spinning—that you love? Sports help kids make friends, stay fit, and enjoy a sense of belonging. Earl Woods said about his son Tiger, "I was using golf to teach him about life. About how to handle responsibility and pressure." Sports can also teach you about team spirit and group effort and doing your best. Says athlete Mia Hamm, "You can't ever live with good enough."

Maybe your favorite extracurricular activity is neither a do-good cause nor a team sport. Maybe you stay after school for chorus or band or chess or stage crew or theater or student council or yearbook committee or Latin Club. No matter what group has you taking the late bus home, being involved beats imagining that you have nothing to do. Being active—physically and otherwise—beats being idle.

*It's better to juggle than to sit on my hands.*

*From there to here, from here to there,*
*funny things are everywhere.*

—Dr. Seuss

❀

Bored? You don't get bored, do you? Restless, tired, weary, challenged, taxed: okay. But not bored. As Robert Louis Stevenson wrote,

> *"The world is so full of a number of things,*
> *I'm sure we should all be as happy as kings."*

Not every moment in life is exciting, but if you're often bored, shake up your routine. Figure out what you can add to your life. Different activities? Different friends? Turn off the TV or computer. Put down the unthrilling thriller. If you get bored, get busy. Because as Eloise, the little girl who lives at the Plaza Hotel, says, "Getting bored is not allowed."

Look for interesting clubs, speakers, contests, and community events. Keep your energy up. "Is giving yourself a pep talk every day silly, superficial, childish? No, on the contrary," wrote Dale Carnegie, "it is the very essence of sound psychology."

Remember, too, that in college you can choose your courses and you may not have to take classes that don't interest you.

**Boredom is beneath me.**

*One does not discover new lands without*
*willingly losing sight of the shore for a very long time.*
—*André Gide*

❀

It took guts for Columbus to sail the ocean blue. But he did it. Now American students routinely travel abroad for summers, semesters, junior years. Some programs, such as the Experiment in International Living and School Year Abroad, arrange for students to live with families in other countries.

Curious about Costa Rica, Canada, China? You decide how far to go in terms of language, distance, and culture.

Adults who have jobs and families can't just pick up and take off. You can. Query your teachers and guidance counselors. Short on funds? Save allowances and earnings and apply for scholarships. When you return, your school and friends will still be there. But you will have new friends, perspectives, and language skills. And no one can take your memories or your adventure away from you. In a Julia Alvarez novel, a character recalls: "These baby monkeys were kept in a cage so long, they wouldn't come out when the doors were finally left open."

Come out. Explore. Let the earth be your classroom. As Mark Twain wrote, "I have never let my schooling interfere with my education."

*To move forward, I have to let go.*

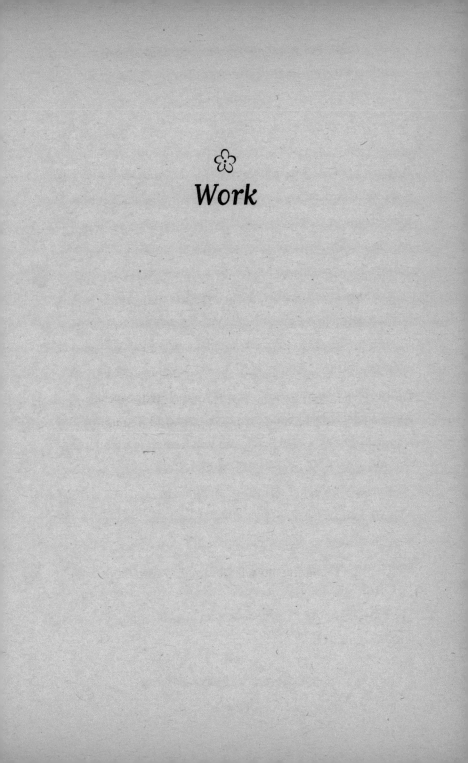

# Work

*Work is more fun than fun.*

—*Noel Coward*

❀

People who are really lucky love working and would keep working even if they won the lottery and could retire. But many are not so lucky. Many don't like their jobs at all and dread going to work each day.

"Work is not man's punishment. It is his reward and his strength, his glory and his pleasure," wrote George Sand. Everyone likes weekends and vacations, but if you are among the fortunate few for whom work is a passion, then someday you will look forward to Mondays as much as Saturdays. (Well, almost.)

For years, everyone has probably been asking you what you were going to be when you grew up. What did you answer? Singer? Doctor? Dancer? Teacher? Actor? Athlete? Have you changed your mind since then? When you're young, you can change your mind again and again as you get to know yourself and the world. As you think about possible careers, consider these words from Whoopi Goldberg: "There are many, many tense adults—we don't need any more tense adults . . . make sure you remember who you are and all the stuff that's made you laugh and dance and jump around."

*Work may be a four-letter word,*
*but it can spell satisfaction.*

*Work is something you can count on,*
*a trusted, lifelong friend who never deserts you.*
——Margaret Bourke-White

❀

If you enjoy taking photographs or playing the harp or writing letters or doing math or meeting new people or traveling or helping others, you can enjoy these pleasures all your life. If you can manage to turn your pleasures into a way of making money, you are blessed indeed. Every job has pros and cons, good days and bad days. But putting your skills to use builds pride.

What are you good at? What do you like to do? Slowly but surely you can aim toward work that interests you. Your future career can be more than a way to make a living; it can be a way to enjoy life.

"Work lovingly done is the secret of all order and all happiness," said Pierre-Auguste Renoir. "If you rest, you rust," said Helen Hayes. Without love, life can seem pretty bleak. But without work, even leisure can feel long. Work—whether at school or a job—can provide structure, focus, meaning, and comfort to your days.

*It feels good to work hard.*

*I started out just wanting to do good work.*

—Jennifer Lopez

❁

What do *you* want to do?

Whether your first job is minding children, waiting tables, or selling jeans, you are learning more than you may realize. If you baby-sit, you're not only perfecting the art of putting on Pampers, you're learning about responsibility and punctuality and how to negotiate money with parents and bedtime with kids. If you're waiting tables, you're sharpening math, memory, and people skills. If you're selling clothes, you're mastering presentation, time management, and how to get along with customers and co-workers. You may also be learning that you don't want to baby-sit or wait tables or be a cashier forever.

Today, your real work may be to do your best at school. In the future, you may work to make money, develop expertise, meet people, help others, realize dreams. Whether you take on a part-time summer job, volunteer internship, or full-time paid position, work is one way in which you define your life. Louisa May Alcott wrote: "Work is and has always been my salvation." Voltaire wrote: "Work spares us from three great evils; boredom, vice, and need."

*Work is the meat and potatoes of life.*

*I have the same goal I've had ever since I was a girl.*
*I want to rule the world.*

*——Madonna*

❀

Are you ambitious? Not everyone is. Some people are more like Ferdinand the bull. Remember him? Ferdinand didn't want to be the fiercest bull in the bullring. He wanted to sit under the cork tree and smell the flowers. And why not?

If, however, you do have larger aspirations, dream them, own them, live them. "I always knew I wanted to be somebody," wrote artist Faith Ringgold. "That's where it begins."

Do you want to be somebody? Who? What do you enjoy doing now that you could enjoy doing forever?

No matter how big or how small your goals, move forward rather than "sit there looking like an envelope without any address on it," as Mark Twain put it. "It's never too late to be what you might have been," wrote George Eliot. And as President John F. Kennedy said, "Once you say you're going to settle for second, that's what happens to you in life, I find."

*Dreams are like live coals. I can let them cool into ash,*
*or fan them until they burn brightly.*

*Get the very best training possible and the doors of*
*opportunity will fly open before you.*
*—W. E. B. DuBois*

❁

If you want something, you have to go after it. Don't wait for the phone to ring. Pick up the receiver yourself. Apply to a good school or college. Tell an employer what you can do and how you can help them. Send out a letter and résumé and follow up with an e-mail or call. A lucky break may come your way, but if no one hands you the perfect job, your job is to go out and find it.

Lauren Bacall said, "The world doesn't owe you a damn thing." Harsh? Yes. But the point is that whether you want to be a tennis star, author, lawyer, doctor, or entrepreneur, it's up to you, not the rest of the world, to make that happen. Apply for positions. Put in the energy. Ask yourself what you are willing to give up to get what you want. Look ahead and plan ahead. Seek mentors or scholarships. Figure out which doors you want to open. In the words of Alice Walker: "Keep in mind always the present you are constructing. It should be the future you want."

**I can climb any ladder.**

*Luck is a matter of preparation meeting opportunity.*

—*Oprah Winfrey*

❀

Every so often, seemingly out of the blue, opportunity will knock. It may not announce itself in an obvious way. It won't say, "Here I am! Your long-awaited opportunity of a lifetime!" It may be far more subtle. Your teacher or neighbor or parent or aunt will make a comment, and suddenly you will realize that there's a job opening (maybe without pay) or a chance to live in Florence (maybe only as a baby-sitter). Or perhaps the lead in the school musical or soprano in the choir or captain of the hockey team will be absent the day of a performance or game, and you will realize (even before the director or coach) that you can save the day. Is this a time for modesty? No. This is a time for action!

A German proverb says: "God gives the nuts, but he does not crack them." Be ready to take advantage of an opportunity. Perhaps you already know someone—a relative or role model—who may be willing and able to make a difference in your life. Think about a job and a paycheck, but also about a career and a life plan.

**When opportunity knocks, I'll have my shoes on.**

*I like that I have a weird life.*

—*Avril Lavigne*

❀

Maybe everything in your life isn't going as planned. And maybe that's okay. Ella Fitzgerald said, "Where there's love and inspiration, I don't think you can go wrong." Montel Williams said, "If you have faith in something bigger than yourself—God, community, family, whatever—then anything is possible."

Can you stand up for your convictions? Or sit down for them? Remember Rosa Parks? She was the black woman who refused to give up her seat to a white man on a bus in Alabama in 1955. She recalled, "He asked if I was going to stand up, and I said, 'No, I'm not.' And he said, 'Well, if you don't stand up, I'm going to . . . call the police and have you arrested.' I said, 'You may do that.'" Next thing you know she'd quietly started the Mongomery Bus Boycott—and made Civil Rights history.

Aviator Amelia Earhart, a headstrong heroine, wrote in a letter: "Please know that I am quite aware of the hazards. I want to do it because I want to do it. Women must try to do things as men have tried. When they fail, their failure must be but a challenge to others."

Do what you have to do.

**This is the time of my life.**

*Those curveballs are always coming—*
*eventually you learn to hit some of them.*
*—Queen Latifah*

❀

Keep swinging and keep your standards high. You may be so good at a certain subject that you can turn in quick work for a great grade. But if you're not an ace at science, isn't that all the more reason to put in extra energy and dazzle yourself as well as the teacher? "What's terrible is to pretend that the second-rate is first-rate. To pretend that you like your work when you know quite well you're capable of better," said Doris Lessing.

"I remember a very important lesson that my father gave me," recalls Nobel Prize winner Toni Morrison. "He said, 'You know, today I welded a perfect seam and I signed my name to it.' And I said, 'But, Daddy, no one's going to see it!' And he said, 'Yeah, but I know it's there.'"

Whether you're baking a pie, running a race, writing a paper, or welding a seam, why do less than your best? Sign your work with pride. Surprise yourself.

I long to accomplish a great and noble task," said Helen Keller, "But it is my chief duty to accomplish small tasks as if they were great and noble."

**If I don't believe in myself, why would others?**

*You can't wait for things to change.*

—*Salma Hayek*

❀

"I don't believe that old cliché that good things come to those who wait. I think good things come to those who want something so bad they can't sit still," said Ashton Kutcher. Thinking big is not enough. "It's plain hard work that does it," wrote inventor Thomas Edison. "Genius," he explained, "is one percent inspiration and ninety-nine percent perspiration."

It helps to be as brilliant as Edison. But even Edison had to buckle down. If you spend time and thought on an essay, it will be better than if you dash it off. If you study for the math test, you'll do better than if you take it cold. If you talk to your teacher or boss, you can make change happen.

Effort pays off, whether as a salary, an invention, better grades, or a better world. As Mary Pipher wrote, "Often what hurts in the short term is ultimately rewarding, while what feels good in the short term is ultimately punishing."

When you work hard, it shows. So heed the advice Yoda gives Luke Skywalker in *The Empire Strikes Back*: "Do—or do not. There is no try."

*If I want to make a difference,*
*I have to make an effort.*

*I still think one of my motivating forces is
to make my mother proud of me.*

—*Nicole Kidman*

❀

Whatever motivates you, persistence and determination are your skeleton keys—the keys that can open any door. Calvin Coolidge said, "Nothing in the world will take the place of persistence. Talent will not; nothing is more common than unsuccessful men with talent. Genius will not; unrewarded genius is almost a proverb. Education will not; the world is full of educated derelicts."

Remember the busy mice in the movie *Cinderella*? Remember how they sang, "We can do it, we can do it, there is really nothing to it"? Remember the blue train in *The Little Engine that Could*? Remember how it huffed and puffed uphill while repeating, "I think I can I think I can I think I can"? Remember the tortoise and the hare in the Aesop story? Remember how slow and steady won the race?

If you give up, it's Game Over. So don't give up. As Josh Billings wrote, "Consider the postage stamp: it's usefulness consists in the ability to stick to one thing till it gets there."

**I can be unstoppable.**

*If you have a passion for something,*
*hold tight and it'll happen.*

*—Ashanti*

❀

Winston Churchill said, "Never never never give up." Give up? You're just getting started. Achievement comes with struggle. The rich and famous all tell stories about the rejections that paved their way. So don't let discouraging or jealous friends block your path. As Mark Twain warned, "Keep away from people who try to belittle your ambitions. Small people always do that, but the really great make you feel that you, too, can become great."

Success won't happen overnight. But if you already know you want to star in a Broadway musical or vault with the Olympic gymnastics team or find a cure for cancer or write the definitive Great American Novel, go for it. Sure it's wise to be realistic. But it's foolish to compromise or back down too soon. So don't fear failure; assume success. As Joseph Campbell advised, "Follow your bliss."

*The mountain looks tall,*
*but I will scale many mountains.*

*In Monroeville, well . . . if they know*
*you are working at home, they think nothing of walking*
*right in for coffee. But they wouldn't dream*
*of interrupting you on the golf course.*

—*Harper Lee*

❀

If you care about what you are reading or writing or memorizing or practicing or learning, why should you put up with endless interruptions? Yes, you have to stop for dinnertime and bedtime. But you don't have to stop working for every phone call or visitor or IM. Put on your away message if every minute matters and you're on-line. Let an answering machine or a family member record your phone calls. Don't be afraid to tell someone that it's a bad time and later would be better. You're allowed to take your work seriously; people will even admire you for it.

As Robert Frost wrote, "The best way out is always through." So minimize distractions and barrel forward. If a deadline or a test or a performance is upon you, make work your top priority. See friends afterward. You'll have more fun because you'll be more relaxed.

*I don't have to apologize for taking my work seriously.*

*Life is improvisation.*

*—Tina Fey*

❁

Persistence counts for a lot, but if it's time to bail, bail. Sometimes it's smart to change your mind and try new things. Maya Angelou wrote, "If you butt your head against a stone wall long enough, at some point you realize the wall is stone and that your head is flesh and blood."

If you've spent two years in a painfully unrequited crush, enough already. *¡Basta y sobra!* If you've invested four years in ballet lessons but they're no longer fun and you're not destined to be a dancer, be glad for the arabesques but cut loose so you can explore and enjoy other endeavors.

Simone de Beauvoir wrote, "In the face of an obstacle which is impossible to overcome, stubbornness is stupid." Don't believe that giving up is always bad. Sometimes giving up one goal may make it possible for you to attain another goal.

**I will be open-minded**
**(but not so open-minded that my brains fall out).**

*Not getting what you want is sometimes*
*a wonderful stroke of luck.*
——*The Dalai Lama*

❀

When you fall short of your goal, you don't have to roll over and play dead. You can get up and keep moving—and give yourself credit for having tried in the first place. Experience is worth more than a trophy. Often the journey is more interesting than the finish line. Said Katharine Hepburn, "As for me, prizes mean nothing. My prize is my work."

Adjust your expectations when necessary, but keep going after what you want. You'll never get the lead if you don't audition. You'll never make the team if you don't try out. You'll never get into that long-shot college if you don't apply. If you don't risk rejection, you don't risk success. "The common idea that success spoils people by making them vain, egotistical, and self-complacent is erroneous," wrote Somerset Maugham. "On the contrary, it makes them, for the most part, humble, tolerant, and kind. Failure makes people cruel and bitter."

*If my goal is still ahead, I have not failed.*

*Woman must not depend upon the protection of man,*
*but must be taught to protect herself.*
—Susan B. Anthony

❀

Henry James wrote, "Summer afternoon—summer afternoon; to me these have always been the most beautiful words in the English language." Dorothy Parker begged to differ: "The two most beautiful words in the English language are 'check enclosed.'"

Work may be its own reward, but it is good to get paid. And it is important to know how to make money and to ask for what you're worth.

Many girls set out to have careers. Others hope to marry men who will be the breadwinners. This plan may pan out . . . but what if the hard-working husband loses his job or dies or asks for a divorce? What if he turns into a cheat or a beast, and the wife wants out? Divorce isn't pretty no matter how you look at it. But divorce with poverty is worse.

Many women remain single or become single, and unless they are born rich, they need to know how to support themselves.

*If I know how to spend money,*
*I had better learn how to make money.*

*Money talks. I hate to listen.*
*But lately it's been screaming in my ear.*
—*Ben Folds*

&#10047;

When you baby-sit or shovel snow or take care of a neighbor's pets or help her clean out her garage, what do you say when she asks, "What do you charge?" Do you shrug, blush, and mumble, "Whatever"? Next time, find out what the going rate is, ask parents and friends for advice, and decide ahead of time what the job is worth to you. Then name your price: "Ten dollars" or "Twenty dollars" or "Five dollars per hour" or "Ten dollars per hour." Be reasonable but sound definite. An employer can always make a counteroffer.

"Ask a lot but take what is offered," says a Russian proverb.

Many people feel awkward about money. Their voices become quiet or high; their sentences sound like questions. But a good worker should be compensated for her labor. Your employer may even respect you more when she sees that you respect yourself and value your time.

During his inaugural address, President John F. Kennedy, speaking on a grander scale, said, "Let us never negotiate out of fear, but let us never fear to negotiate."

*I will ask for what I think I deserve.*

*He who obtains has little.*

*He who scatters has much.*

—*Lao Tzu*

❁

There's nothing wrong with obtaining things. But the mall is not the be-all and end-all. In Arthur Miller's play *The Price*, a character says, "Years ago a person, he was unhappy, didn't know what to do with himself—he'd go to church, start a revolution—*something*. Today you're unhappy? Can't figure it out? What is the salvation? Go shopping."

Sarah Jessica Parker says, "I'm not my character. I don't want people to think I spend the better part of the day deciding where to shop." What about you? Do you spend too much time shopping? Some teenagers ruin their credit ratings by mistaking credit cards for blank checks. Others flash debit cards—and abracadabra—their savings disappear.

When you do shop, be careful. Take advantage of sales, but if the shirt is no-return, make sure it fits and has no missing buttons. No matter how cute, patient, or insistent the clerk is, if you don't want it, don't buy it. And at the grocer's, check expiration dates. Why spend today's money on yesterday's milk?

*I won't spend big money on little nothings.*

*Save money and money will save you.*

—*Jamaican proverb*

❁

Sophie Tucker said, "I've been rich and I've been poor. Rich is better." Most everyone would agree. It's good to have money and to know how to make more.

Yet the Bible says, "The love of money is the root of all evil." If money starts complicating your relationships or compromising your values, that's not good. Borrowing or lending money can sabotage friendships. And choosing companions because they are rich is shallow and can leave you feeling lonely.

Do wealthy people have the most fun? Not necessarily. Tennis champion Martina Navratilova points out, "The rich guys buy a football team, the poor guys buy a football. It's all relative."

If you have no dollars to spare, it can be hard to believe that rich people aren't happy all the time. But rich people can get used to caviar and fancy cars as fast as the rest of us can get used to hot dogs and bicycles. And rich people, like all people, have worries, troubles, and unfulfilled dreams of their own.

While money helps, it cannot buy time or love or happiness.

**The bottom line is important but so is the rest of the page.**

*The trouble with being in the rat race is that*
*even if you win, you're still a rat.*

—Lily Tomlin

❀

Money is a motivator, and right now you might do backflips just to land a job at minimum wage. Fine. Once you're hired, don't get fired. Work efficiently and independently. Speak up if you don't understand a task. Accept responsibility if you make a mistake. Be friendly; give compliments; say thank-you to your boss, co-workers, customers. Be zealous and don't bound out the door at five sharp as though you're a puppy who has to piddle.

Let's say you're such a good worker that you get promoted and promoted and promoted. Congratulations! But keep an eye on the big picture. Is this your chosen field? Even if you make a lot of money, be sure you enjoy how you make it and don't let money tarnish your values. Brooke Shields, who became rich as a teen model, said, "People ask, 'Why did you go to college?' I never considered not going to college." Paul Simon said, "Fame is a very dangerous acquisition. . . . If you do get it, use it to help others. Otherwise, it can be poisonous."

*I can balance what I have to do with what I want to do.*

*Many a man thinks he is making something*
*when he's only changing things around.*
—*Zora Neale Hurston*

❀

Did you ever read *Miss Rumphius*? It's about an old woman who thinks, "But there is still one more thing I have to do. I have to make the world more beautiful." And she does. She plants the fields and hillsides of her seaside home with blue- and purple- and rose-colored lupines that bloom year after year.

How can you improve your world? Through flowers? Through politics?

Playwright Tony Kushner wrote, "If you're gay and you can't hold hands, or you're black and you can't catch a taxi, or you're a woman and you can't go into the park, you are aware there's a menace. The world should be striving to make all its members secure."

How can you strive to make the world better?

Noel Coward wrote, "Self-respect cannot be purchased. It is never for sale. It comes to us when we are alone, in quiet moments, in quiet places, when we suddenly realize that, knowing the good, we have done it; knowing the beautiful, we have served it; knowing the truth, we have spoken it."

*The world is not perfect; I can try to make it better.*

*Oh, it was my mother's idea.*

*It wasn't like I asked to be in the business!*

—Bernadette Peters

❁

Bernadette Peters performed at Carnegie Hall at age four and has been a successful star of stage and screen ever since. Did her mom push her? Yes. But Peters loves entertaining, so those pushes turned out to be a good thing.

Of course, parental pushes are not always so welcome. Are yours pushing you where you don't want to go? Maybe your dad is a world-class cellist and wants you to go pro with music. Maybe your mom is a lawyer who wants you to go to law school. Fine—if you want to.

But if you do not want to go down that road, you don't have to. After all, if you realize *their* aspirations rather than your own, later you may feel resentful or haunted by what-ifs.

John Malkovich said, "If you talked about success and money around my father, he would have knocked your teeth out. He wanted us to be good at what we did. And certainly money would not be the goal."

What are your parents' goals for you? What are yours for yourself?

**I will find my path.**

*A little rebellion is a good thing.*

—*Thomas Jefferson*

❀

All work and no play makes Jack a dull boy—and doesn't do much for Jill, either. Give yourself a break. Get some sunshine and hang out with friends. Study breaks and work breaks aren't perks—they're necessities! "The time you enjoy wasting is not wasted time," wrote Bertrand Russell.

When you work, work hard. But afterward, relax. There is no need to burn yourself out or to meet impossible standards or to make tons of money. You don't have to pay the rent yet, right? Don't pressure yourself unduly. Chill out. Take walks. Take naps. Play games. Call friends. See movies. You're entitled to gather your rosebuds as well as your report cards and paychecks.

You're getting stressed, overwhelmed, exhausted? Here's Lily Tomlin's remedy: "For fast-acting relief, try slowing down." And Henry Wadsworth Longfellow wrote, "Youth comes but once in a lifetime."

**On the seventh day, even God put Her feet up.**

# Parting Words

*An adult is an obsolete child.*

*——Dr. Seuss*

❀

*All children, except one, grow up. They soon know that they will grow up, and the way Wendy knew was this. One day when she was two years old, she was playing in a garden, and she plucked another flower and ran with it to her mother. I suppose she must have looked rather delightful, for Mrs. Darling put her hand to her heart and cried, "Oh, why can't you remain like this forever!" This was all that passed between them on the subject, but henceforth Wendy knew that she must grow up. You always know after you are two. Two is the beginning of the end.*

So begins J. M. Barrie's *Peter Pan*. And so begins the last chapter of this book. Being a child is wonderful, but being your age can be even better. You're old enough to pick your own music and friends and activities. Yet you're not too old to enjoy cartwheels, cartoons, revolving doors, banana splits, rainbows, kittens, even snowball fights. And why should you ever be?

In 1897, an eight-year-old girl wrote to the editor of *The New York Sun* and asked, "Is there a Santa Claus?" His wise reply: "Yes, Virginia, there is a Santa Claus. He exists as certainly as love and generosity and devotion exist. . . . How dreary would be the world if there were no Santa Claus!"

**I can grow up, not old.**

*A child's world is fresh and new and beautiful, full of wonder and excitement. It is our misfortune that for most of us, that clear-eyed vision, that true instinct for what is beautiful and awe-inspiring, is dimmed and even lost before we reach adulthood.*

—*Rachel Carson*

❀

When was the last time you looked at a tree or a leaf or a flower or even a work of art and were astounded by its beauty? When is the last time you looked at the world with a child's eyes—or even a tourist's eyes—and felt surprised and uplifted?

In E. B. White's *Charlotte's Web*, everyone gives advice to Wilbur the pig. The spider says, "Slowly, slowly! Never hurry and never worry!" The goose says, "Run all over! Skip and dance, jump and prance! . . . The world is a wonderful place when you're young."

The world is a wonderful place no matter how old you are. But it helps if you can retain your sense of wonder and remember to skip and dance. "I finally figured out the only reason to be alive is to enjoy it," wrote Rita Mae Brown.

*I will enjoy the time of my life.*

*Life is what happens to you*
*when you're making other plans.*
—*John Lennon*

❀

Patricia MacLachlan wrote in a novel, "He never learned that most things are only there for a moment, quite perfect and fine, like snow." Have you learned that some things don't last?

Do you notice your surroundings? Do you enjoy your routine—and the moments that break up your routine? Do you love your family? Your friends? The stuff of your life? Do you relish what you have instead of always yearning for more?

"A lot of people get caught up looking so far down the road that they miss what's right in front of them," said rapper Nelly.

"One cannot collect all the beautiful shells on the beach. One can collect only a few, and they are the most beautiful if they are few," wrote Anne Morrow Lindbergh. This Yiddish proverb strikes a grimmer note: "Shrouds are made without pockets." Translation: You can't take it with you. But you can enjoy yourself today, can't you?

*I will not just be alive; I will be aware.*

*Seize the day.*

——*Horace*

❁

Do you know people who say, "I can't wait until Thanksgiving," or "I can't wait until I'm older"? No matter how bright your future, why wish away today? Do you know people who say "Thank God it's Friday" or "I have an hour to kill"? Why dismiss Monday, Tuesday, Wednesday, or Thursday? Why kill time when you can't make more of it?

"Youth is wasted on the young," George Bernard Shaw wrote. But not your youth. You're paying attention. And while it's impossible to live each day to the fullest, to enjoy each hour to the hilt, to make each minute count, you recognize that as a worthy goal. "Today is always gone tomorrow," wrote Wislawa Szymborska, a Polish poet who won the Nobel prize.

Emily Dickinson wrote, "That it will never come again, is what makes life so sweet." Do you find time for fun and for work? Pleasure and purpose? You can't do it all, but you can do what you can. "If I got hit by a bus," said George Clooney, "I'd want people to say, 'He jammed it all in.' That's my driving force."

**Seize the day . . . squeeze the moment.**

*I hate waiting around. I like to make it happen.*
*I'm not a control freak—well, I probably am.*

—*Drew Barrymore*

Madonna said, "You have to be patient. I'm not." For better or worse, most of us do learn patience. You can't rush prom night or summer vacation or Christmas or Hanukkah or friendship or fitness or love or happiness or wisdom. You can try to move in the right direction. You can try to stay healthy and strong. You can try to make your days meaningful and to listen to the YES inside and outside you. But you can't hurry your life along. So why not savor it? Why not take your time getting older?

As Ursula K. LeGuin put it, "It is good to have an end to journey toward; but it is the journey that matters, in the end." Adlai Stevenson wrote, "It's not the years in our life but the life in your years that counts."

And Rainer Maria Rilke wrote, "Being an artist means not reckoning and counting, but ripening like the tree which does not force its sap. Patience is everything!"

**Learning patience requires patience.**

*No one tests the depth of a river with two feet.*

—*African proverb*

❀

"Look twice before you leap," concurs Charlotte Brontë. Doing things carefully and well makes more sense than doing things in a slapdash way, impulsively, or incorrectly. "Better to ask twice than lose your way once," goes a Danish proverb.

Better, too, to leave an extra fifteen minutes to get to the airport than to sweat out every red light. Even if you're just going to a movie or meeting friends, leave early so you arrive on time. Bring a book or diary or cell phone, if you get there first, you can always read or write or call someone.

You can choose to be punctual, not frantic; organized not overwhelmed; careful, not careless. Piet Hein wrote a poem that could be engraved on too many tombstones:

> *Here lies, extinguished in his prime,*
> *a victim of modernity:*
> *but yesterday he hadn't time—*
> *and now he has eternity.*

**I will give myself the time I need.**

*I never travel without my diary.*
*One should always have something sensational*
*to read in the train.*
—Oscar Wilde

❀

Do you have a diary? A diary is a friend who listens, and writing down your thoughts and observations can help you discover what matters to you—and help you keep things in perspective. Are you worried that you're penning drivel or just whining on paper? Keep writing. Your best words will come. A diary accepts both self-pity and brilliant insights. Are you worried instead about privacy? Trust your family—but hide your diary!

Someday you may look back on your diary with embarrassment. Is that the best you could spell? Did you really have a crush on *him*? Don't discard old diaries. Reread them. They'll show the arc of who you were and who you have become. Revisiting one's childhood and adolescence is one of the worthy diversions of adulthood. Plato wrote, "The life which is unexamined is not worth living." Milan Kundera asked, "You think that just because it's already happened, the past is finished and unchangeable? Oh no, the past is cloaked in multicolored taffeta and every time we look at it we see a different hue."

*I can time travel through my own life.*

*Into each life, some rain must fall,*
*Some days must be dark and dreary.*
—Henry Wadsworth Longfellow

❀

Nothing is perfect, and bad hair days (as well as true travails) are inevitable. But dreary days help us appreciate bright ones. Because things are terrible today doesn't mean that they will stay terrible. Sometimes you have to undergo arduous training to achieve a fabulous performance. Sometimes you have to survive a wrenching breakup to get to the winning relationship.

If you bomb a test, that doesn't mean you'll flunk the course. If your friends turn on you, that doesn't mean you'll spend your life alone. Even if there is real heartbreak, there will still be joys ahead.

Someday you may even be able to convert your worst experiences into art. As John Ciardi wrote, "You don't have to suffer to be a poet. Adolescence is enough suffering for anyone." As a character in an A. R. Gurney play puts it, "Life has taught me this: even if the main course is somewhat disappointing, there's always dessert."

*Without bees and rain: no flowers, no rainbows.*

*I like living. I have sometimes been wildly,*
*despairingly, acutely miserable, racked with sorrow,*
*but through it all I still know quite certainly*
*that just to be alive is a grand thing.*

—*Agatha Christie*

❀

Things will look different tomorrow. Things will be better soon. There are adults who can help you. If you want to change your life, you can. And as Alice Walker put it: "Life is better than death, I believe, if only because it is less boring, and because it has fresh peaches in it."

Everybody despairs at some point. Calderón de la Barca wrote, "No unhappiness is equal to that of anticipating unhappiness." But people forgive; new friends and boyfriends come along; situations turn out better than you thought they would. You are also more resilient than you think. You have inner resources that you haven't yet tapped. Albert Camus wrote, "In the midst of winter, I finally learned that there was in me an invincible summer."

Time itself can make a difference. "If Winter comes," Percy Bysshe Shelley asked, "can Spring be far behind?"

*Moods are like seasons: They change.*

*Regret is an appalling waste of energy;*
*you can't build on it; it's only good for wallowing in.*
—*Katherine Mansfield*

❀

Edith Piaf, a tiny French singer, belted out, *"Je ne regrette rien."* ("I regret nothing.") William Maxwell, when nearing ninety wrote, "I have regrets but there are not very many of them and, fortunately, I forget what they are."

Everyone sifts through memories. Some people regret things they said or did. Others regret things they didn't say or do. If you have a habit of second-guessing yourself, make an effort to learn from the past but to connect to the present. "Life must be understood backwards," wrote Søren Kierkegaard, "but . . . . it must be lived forwards."

Consider this verse by Piet Hein:

*The road to wisdom?——Well, it's plain*
*and simple to express:*
*Err*
*And err*
*And err again*
*But less*
*And less*
*And less.*

**I can look back, but I will move forward.**

*If I have lost the ring,*
*I still have the fingers.*
—*Italian proverb*

❀

There is always another way of looking at things. Deep in the Hundred Acre Wood, Winnie the Pooh was once planning to give Eeyore a jar of honey for his birthday. But the chubby cubby got hungry and licked the jar clean before realizing his mistake. Did he feel awful? No. Ever the optimist, Pooh examined the empty jar and said, "I'm very glad that I thought of giving you a Useful Pot to put things in." Eeyore was glad, too. What he wanted, after all, was just to be remembered on his birthday.

Yes, you're bummed that you lost a five-dollar bill. But think how pleased the person who finds it will be. Yes, you're upset that you misplaced your prized blue ribbon. But you'll never forget what it felt like to win.

You can't always give troubles a positive spin. But when things look bleak, look again. Many sorry situations work out for the best. Shift your camera angle and you might find something to salvage—or even celebrate.

*I will ask myself:*
*Is there another way of looking at this?*

*Do not be breakin' a shin on a stool*
*that's not in your path.*
——*Irish proverb*

❀

Do you invent problems? Are you an alarmist? If you can't find your keys or glasses or purse, they probably aren't lost forever. They're probably on the bureau in the next room. If your sister is ten minutes late returning from the store, she probably didn't have an accident. She probably ran one more errand.

Your life has enough stress without your panicking prematurely and creating more. If you're going out with someone you like, why obsess that he might break up with you? If you're a good student, why worry that the next test will do you in? Why cry yourself to sleep over an ex-friend or a lost crush? It makes more sense to dry your eyes and make more friends——female and male.

The Italians have a proverb: "There is no rose without thorns." It's true——even the Lady Banksia rose, which is called thornless, has tiny thorns. But why be so anxious about thorns that you overlook a rose's beauty and fragrance? And if you ever do have a thorn in your side? Take it out and toss it away.

*I will be an optimist—with an umbrella.*

*I hate housework! You make the beds, you do the dishes—*
*and six months later you have to start all over again.*

—Joan Rivers

❦

Is your room so tidy it could be photographed? Skip this page. Is your room a disaster area (even if you know where the essentials are)? Take action.

Matsushita Konosuke, founder of Panasonic, said, "It is necessary to approach a project with the conviction that it *can* be done, and not waste energy worrying about its difficulty." Instead of despairing because your room is beyond-belief messy, start straightening it up. It's a big job, but it's doable.

Once you decide to organize rather than agonize, tackle the task methodically. Begin by making your bed in the morning—you can do it when you're still half asleep. Sort through drawers one at a time, putting away or throwing away the contents. What's that pile on your desk? Move it to the kitchen table and decide which papers go where. You've outgrown some clothes? Give them away. You want to save last year's reports? Okay, but must they be front and center in your work space? File, file, file!

**It's as easy to drape jeans over a hanger**
**as it is to drape them over a chair.**

*It rots the senses in the head!*
*It kills imagination dead!*
—*Roald Dahl*

❀

"Television is an invention that permits you to be entertained in your living room by people you wouldn't have in your home," wrote David Frost.

Television isn't all bad. There are nature programs, documentaries, sitcoms, and other shows that help you learn and laugh and relax. Nonetheless, Lily Tomlin points out, "If you read a lot, you're considered well-read. But if you watch a lot of TV, you're not considered well-viewed." Groucho Marx goes further: "I must say I find television very educational. The minute somebody turns it on, I go into the library and read a good book."

When is television a problem? When it's always on. When you find yourself watching whatever is offered rather than choosing particular programs. When you start to want what commercials tell you to want. When you blow off doing homework or sports because it's easy to sprawl on the couch, potato-like. When you can't think of anything to do with a friend besides watch the tube. When you stop having friends because it's easier to have a one-way relationship with the "idiot box."

*I can turn the TV on . . . and off.*

*We do not inherit the land from our ancestors;*
*we borrow it from our children.*

—*Native American proverb*

❀

Elizabeth Barrett Browning wrote: "Earth's crammed with heaven." But Samuel Johnson said, "Hell is paved with good intentions." Many people are all for waving the green flag of ecology. Then they litter, reach for paper towels instead of a sponge, or let cashiers put tiny purchases into bags instead of putting the item and receipt directly into their purse or backpack.

Even if you're not on a committee to save the rain forest, adopt a highway, or clean up city parks, you can do your part for the environment. "Something is better than nothing," wrote Lady Bird Johnson, a former First Lady and the founder of the Wildflower Center that bears her name. Every effort counts. Recycle. Think twice before buying Styrofoam cups or plastic forks, flushing the toilet for mere tissue, leaving lights on when you exit a room, turning up the heat when you could put on a sweater, blasting the air-conditioning when you could open a window. Perhaps your family can afford all this. But your planet can't.

**I won't be wasteful.**

> *The Earth is crying out to us.*
>
> *And so few of us are actually listening.*
>
> —Stevie Wonder

❧

You can't vote yet. But your actions make a difference. Study the label on a can of tuna. Were nets used that could harm dolphins? Do you buy organic food? The fewer pesticides out there, the better (for you *and* the world). How about unbleached flour, recycled paper, less heavily packaged foods? Newman's Own popcorn is delicious, and profits go to philanthropic causes. Buy from companies with a conscience! Why support corporations that use child labor when other businesses strive to hire disadvantaged adults? If you're glad your town has a corner bookstore, pharmacy, or mom-and-pop diner, shop there. Let your money reflect your values. Write to politicians and executives. Inform friends. Make your voice heard. "Whether you want it or not," wrote Wislawa Szymborska, "you walk with political steps on political ground." In 430 B.C., Pericles said, "Just because you do not take an interest in politics doesn't mean politics won't take an interest in you." More recently, Kofi Annan of the U.N. said, "Issues that once seemed very far away are very much in your backyard."

**I can be complacent—or committed.**

*We have just enough religion to make us hate,*

*but not enough to make us love one another.*

—*Jonathan Swift*

❀

Do you believe in God? Are you Catholic or Protestant or Jewish or Muslim or Buddhist? Is worship part of your life?

Some people who are not religious cannot understand those who are. And some devoutly religious people have zero tolerance for those who don't share their beliefs.

"The problem with writing about religion is that you run the risk of offending seriously religious people, and then they come after you with machetes," wrote humorist Dave Barry. "So I am going to be very sensitive, here, which is not easy, because the thing about religion is that everybody else's always appears stupid."

Cross yourself, keep kosher, bow to Mecca—or don't. But don't make fun of people who worship differently from you—or who don't worship at all. You can choose for yourself how religion does or does not fit into your personal life. But it's important for us all to try to respect other people's beliefs and cultures.

*I can respect people who are different from me.*

*Take anything you're told as a suggestion,*
*not solid advice. You have to do what works for you.*
*—Sandra Bullock*

❀

"The problem with good advice is that it's hard to follow," says my character Melanie Martin in her third diary. Marie Curie, Nobel Prize winner, wrote, "Nothing in life is to be feared. It is only to be understood." But who understands *everything*? Not authors. Not scientists. Not therapists. Not teachers. Not poets. Not friends. Not advice columnists.

Some people have more insight and sense than others, but common sense is not common. And there is no rule book, or answer sheet. Gertrude Stein wrote, "There ain't no answer. There ain't going to be any answer. There never has been an answer. That's the answer."

At times you may not know how to finish a short story. Or where to go to college. Or which guy to get serious with. Others may offer opinions. But the decision will be yours. East Coast or West Coast? David or Daniel? Take your time, and take comfort in knowing that sometimes there can be more than one right answer, and you can change your mind.

*Door #1, #2, or #3?*
*It really is up to me.*

*Too many people seem to think life is a spectator sport.*

—*Katharine Hepburn*

❀

Many people wade through life without making conscious choices. "To live is the rarest thing in the world," wrote Oscar Wilde. "Most people just exist."

You are not most people. You are taking the time to think and to consider the thoughts of wise (and otherwise) men and women born long before you. You are moving from confusion to confidence. And you are beginning to appreciate and believe in yourself.

"To be what we are, and to become what we are becoming, is the only end in life," wrote Robert Louis Stevenson.

You are becoming yourself. You are going places. You are living your life—passionately, not passively. "A dead thing can go with the stream," wrote G. K. Chesterton, "but only a living thing can go against it."

*I can lead my life instead of being led by it.*

*The ripest peach is on the highest tree.*

—James Whitcomb Riley

❀

Some girls lose their balance during these fast-changing years. Others hit their stride. Think about what you want your life to be like. Who you want to be. What you want to accomplish.

"It's not enough to be industrious; so are the ants—what are you industrious about?" asked Henry David Thoreau. Many adults are set in their ways, entrenched in their careers. You are still free to choose your path.

If you have worthy goals, it will take time and energy to realize them. You have time and energy. Don't listen to naysayers. Squelch the voice inside you that whispers that you can't do it. You *can* do it. You can!

Abraham Lincoln said, "Things may come to those who wait—but only the things left by those who hustle."

Are you willing to hustle? Are you willing to wrestle with your demons? Willing to let your angels hit the high notes?

Give it your all. Because life doesn't start at graduation. It has already started.

**Watch out, world, here I come!**

❀

# *Your Favorite Quotations*

*Now this is not the end.*

*It is not even the beginning of the end.*

*But it is, perhaps, the end of the beginning.*

——*Winston Churchill*

An artist never really finishes his work.
He merely abandons it.

—Paul Valéry

✿

*Never think you've seen the last of anything.*

—*Eudora Welty*

*Ends and beginnings—there are no such things.*

*There are only middles.*

—Robert Frost

*Endings have always been hard for me.*

—Judy Blume

*Eternity's a terrible thought.*
*I mean, where's it all going to end?*
—*Tom Stoppard*

*Our revels now are ended.*

—*William Shakespeare*

*That's all folks!*

—*Porky Pig*

# Index

Aesop, 47, 146

Affleck, Ben, 81

African American spiritual, 10

African proverbs, 36, 109, 166

Aguilera, Christina, 12

Albert I (king of England), 116

Alcott, Lousia May, 139

Alfred, Tennyson, Lord, 83

Alvarez, Julia, 134

Andersen, Hans Christian, 18

Angelou, Maya, 127, 149

Aniston, Jennifer, 18, 33

Annan, Kofi, 176

Anthony, Susan B., 151

Arbus, Diane, 73

Archer, Isabel (*The Portrait of a Lady* character), 12

Aristotle, 99, 129

Armstrong, Lance, 93

Ashanti, 147

Astor, Nancy, 26

Austen, Jane, 44

Bacall, Lauren, 141

Bacon, Francis, 33

Baez, Joan, 56

Barca, Calderón de la, 169

Barrie, J. M., 161

Barry, Dave, 177

Barrymore, Drew, 165

Barzun, Jacques, 115

Baum, L. Frank, 82

Beauvoir, Simone de, 76, 149

Bergen, Candice, 68

Bergess, Gelett, 21

Berry, Halle, 15

Bhagavad Gita, 41

Bible quotes, 24, 40, 75, 109, 154

Billings, Josh, 146

Blume, Judy, 187

Borges, Jorge Luis, 63

Bourke-White, Margaret, 138

Bradbury, Ray, 124

Brontë, Charlotte, 166

Brooks, Mel, 23

Brown, Helen Gurley, 17

Brown, Rita Mae, 162

Browning, Elizabeth Barrett, 175

Buck, Pearl S., 92

Buddha, 15

Bullock, Sandra, 178

Burns, George, 90

Butler, Samuel, 8, 57, 110

Campbell, Joseph, 147

Camus, Albert, 169

Carnegie, Dale, 37, 133

Carroll, Lewis, 2

Carson, Rachel, 162

Catherine II (queen of England), 42

Caulfield, Holden (*The Catcher in the Rye* character), 121

Cervantes, Miguel de, 2, 20

*Charlotte's Web* (White), 131, 162

Cher, 15

Chesterton, G. K., 72, 179

Chinese proverbs, 49, 70, 106, 118, 123

Chisholm, Shirley, 131

Christie, Agatha, 22, 169

Churchill, Jennie Jerome, 12

Churchill, Winston, 66, 147, 183

Ciardi, John, 168

*Cinderella*, 146

Clark, Mary Higgins, 23

Clinton, Bill, 95

Clinton, Hillary Rodham, 94

Clooney, George, 164

Colette, 40, 94, 124

Confucius, 11

Congreve, William, 78

Coolidge, Calvin, 116, 146

Cortázar, Julio, 131

Cosby, Bill, 13, 98

Couric, Katie, 52

Coward, Noel, 137, 156

Crawford, Cindy, 17

Creole proverb, 51

Cruise, Tom, 7

Curie, Marie, 178

Curtis, Jamie Lee, 6

Dahl, Roald, 20, 174

The Dalai Lama, 150

Danish proverbs, 13, 166

Davis, Miles, 128

Descartes, René, 123

Diaz, Cameron, 41

Dickinson, Emily, 34, 164

Dietrich, Marlene, 69

Dinesen, Isak, 28

Dior, Christian, 19

Dostoyevsky, Fyodor, 97

Dr. Seuss, 133, 161

DuBois, W. E. B., 141

Earhart, Amelia, 143

Edison, Thomas, 145

Einstein, Albert, 126

Eliot, George, 76, 140

Eliot, T. S., 122

Elizabeth I (queen of England), 22

Eloise (character), 133

Emerson, Ralph Waldo, 21, 35

Epictetus, 74

Euclid, 120

Euripides, 56

Faiz, Faiz Ahmed, 74

Fey, Tina, 13, 149

Fields, Sally, 13

Fitzgerald, Ella, 143

Flaubert, Gustave, 124

Folds, Ben, 16, 152

Ford, Henry, 112

Frank, Anne, 36
Franklin, Ben, 20, 46, 117
Freud, Anna, 121
Freud, Sigmund, 71
Frost, David, 174
Frost, Robert, 29, 148, 174, 186

Gallant, Mavis, 106
Gandhi, Indira, 29
Gandhi, Mahatma, 100
*Gentlemen Prefer Blondes* (Jane
    Russell's character), 42
German proverbs, 39, 81, 142
Gibran, Kahlil, 77
Gide, André, 134
Glass, Julia, 82
Glover, Danny, 130
Goethe, 9, 94, 122
Goldberg, Whoopi, 137
Goldsworthy, Andy, 126
Grafton, Sue, 120
*The Great Gatsby* (Fitzgerald), 42
Guiterman, Arthur, 66
Gurney, A. R., 168

Hamm, Mia, 132
Hayek, Salma, 145
Hayes, Helen, 138
Hein, Piet, 166, 170
Hellman, Lillian, 55
Hemingway, Ernst, 78
Hepburn, Katharine, 150, 179
Hillary, Sir Edmund, 116
Hindu proverb, 11
Hitchcock, Alfred, 115

Holiday, Billie, 27, 63
Homer, 15
Horace, 164
Hornby, Nick, 55
Howell III, Thurston (*Gilligan's
    Island* character), 19
Hugo, Victor, 105
Hungerford, Margaret Wolfe, 14
Hurston, Zora Neale, 34, 156

India.Arie, 14
Indian proverb, 53
Irish proverb, 172
Irving, Washington, 108
Italian proverbs, 171, 172

Jackson, Jesse, 40
Jamaican proverbs, 42, 154
James, Henry, 12, 151
James, William, 38
James I (king of England), 25
Japanese proverbs, 36, 116
Jefferson, Thomas, 158
Jesus, 40
Johnson, Lady Bird, 175
Johnson, Samuel, 175
Jo (*Little Women* character), 90
Jong, Erica, 127

Kabbalah quote, 22
Kafka, Franz, 124
Kashmir saying, 57
Keillor, Garrison, 99
Keller, Helen, 130, 144
Kennedy, John F., 140, 152

Kern, Jerome, 56
Kidman, Nicole, 113, 146
Kierkegaard, Søren, 170
King, Carole, 24
King, Martin Luther, Jr., 48, 79
Knowles, Beyoncé, 82
Konosuke, Matsushita, 173
Kreuk, Kristin, 51
Kudrow, Lisa, 120
Kundera, Milan, 167
Kushner, Tony, 156
Kutcher, Ashton, 96, 145

La Fontaine, Jean de, 54
Lamott, Anne, 35
Larsen, Gary, 197
Latifah, Queen, 144
Lauren, Ralph, 19
Lavigne, Avril, 143
Lebanese proverb, 46
Lebowitz, Fran, 103
Lee, Harper, 148
LeGuin, Ursula K., 79, 165
Leguizamo, John, 18
L'Engle, Madeleine, 113
Lennon, John, 163
Lessing, Doris, 144
Letterman, David, 51
Lin, Maya, 108
Lincoln, Abraham, 50, 180
Lindbergh, Anne Morrow, 163
The Little Engine That Could, 146
Longfellow, Henry Wadsworth,
    158, 168
Lopez, Jennifer, 73, 139

Loren, Sophia, 128

MacLachlan, Patricia, 163
Madonna, 140, 165
Malcolm X, 123
Malkovich, John, 157
Mandela, Nelson, 98
Mansfield, Katherine, 170
Maria (West Side Story character), 17
Martin, Steve, 2
Markham, Beryl, 6
Márquez, Garbriel García, 107
Marquis, Don, 117
Martin, Melanie (character), 178
Marx, Groucho, 174
Mason, Jackie, 114
Matthew (apostle), 24, 40
Matthews, Dave, 8
Maugham, Somerset, 47, 150
Maxwell, William, 170
McCartney, Paul, 91
Mead, Margaret, 89
Midler, Bette, 18
Miller, Arthur, 153
Miss Rumphius, 156
Molière, 12
Montesquieu, 123
Montessori, Maria, 113
Morissette, Alanis, 7
Morley, Christopher, 95
Morrison, Toni, 41, 144
Mother Teresa, 99
Moynihan, Daniel Patrick, 125
Munch, Edvard, 80
Murdoch, Iris, 64

Myers, Mike, 9

Nabokov, Vladimir, 125
Native American proverb, 175
Navratilova, Martina, 154
Nelly, 163
Neruda, Pablo, 83
Nevelson, Louise, 22
*The New York Sun* editorial, 161
Nietzsche, Freidrich, 62
Nin, Anaïs, 38

O'Brien, Conan, 130
O'Keeffe, Georgia, 126
O'Neal, Shaquille, 89, 132
Orwell, George, 28
Ovid, 15, 66

Pacino, Al, 26
Paltrow, Gwyneth, 8
Parker, Dorothy, 9, 75, 151
Parker, Sarah Jessica, 115, 153
Parks, Rosa, 143
Parton, Dolly, 64
Pascal, Blaise, 70
Penn, William, 37
Pericles, 176
*Peter Pan*, 161
Peters, Bernadette, 157
Piaf, Edith, 170
Picasso, Pablo, 126
Pickford, Mary, 128
Pink Floyd, 112
Pipher, Mary, 16, 145
Plato, 1, 167

Polish proverb, 92
Polonius (Shakespeare character), 119
Porky Pig (character), 190
Price, Leontyne, 23
*The Price* (Miller), 153

Quindlen, Anna, 84, 115

Radner, Gilda, 19
Rainey, Ma, 81
Renoir, Pierre-Auguste, 138
Rhea, Caroline, 131
Riley, James Whitcome, 180
Rilke, Rainer Maria, 77, 165
Ringgold, Faith, 140
Rivers, Joan, 173
Rogers, Will, 101, 128
Roosevelt, Eleanor, 11, 52
Rowling, J.K., 50
Russell, Bertrand, 158
Russian proverb, 152

St. Paul, 75
St. Vincent Millay, Edna, 65
Salinger, J. D., 121, 122
Sand, George, 137
Sandburg, Carl, 113
Santana, Carlos, 91
Santayana, George, 38
Sarton, May, 107
Schulz, Charles, 100, 110
Scottish proverb, 80
*The Secret Life of Bees*, 95
Seinfeld, Jerry, 102

Shakespeare, William, 51, 65, 75, 119, 189

Shaw, George Bernard, 164

Shelley, Percy Bysshe, 169

Shields, Brooke, 155

Simon, Paul, 155

Singer, Isaac Bashevis, 125

Socrates, 7

Sontag, Susan, 123

Sophocles, 61, 129

Starr, Ringo, 39

*Star Trek*, 29

Stein, Gertrude, 6, 26, 178

Steinbeck, John, 74

Steinem, Gloria, 6, 109

Stevenson, Adlai, 165

Stevenson, Robert Louis, 133, 179

Stoppard, Tom, 188

Swift, Jonathan, 177

Syrus, Publilius, 96

Szymborska, Wislawa, 164, 176

Talmud, 78

Tharp, Twyla, 124

Thayer, Nancy, 125

Thomas, Dylan, 107

Thoreau, Henry David, 29, 101, 180

Thurber, James, 85

Timberlake, Justin, 81

Tomlin, Lily, 62, 155, 158, 174

Trudeau, Garry, 29

Trudeau, Margaret, 104

Truman, Harry, 110

Tucker, Sophie, 154

Twain, Mark, 70, 94, 117, 119, 134, 140, 147

Tzu, Lao, 153

Unamuno, Miguel de, 122

Valéry, Paul, 184

Victoria (queen of England), 40

Voltaire, 104, 139

Walker, Alice, 84, 141, 169

Walters, Barbara, 46

Welty, Eudora, 185

Wharton, Edith, 55

White, E. B., 53, 118, 131, 162, 192

Whitman, Walt, 8, 121

Wilde, Oscar, 5, 45, 67, 167, 179

Williams, Montel, 143

Williams, Serena, 100

Williams, Vanessa, 7

Williams, Venus, 120

Williamson, Marianne, 10

Winfrey, Oprah, 9, 23, 123, 142

Winnie the Pooh (character), 171

Witherspoon, Reese, 43, 93

Wolfe, Tom, 56

Wonder, Stevie, 176

Woods, Earl, 132

Wright, Frank Lloyd, 10

Wyse, Lois, 114

Yeats, William Butler, 112

Yiddish proveb, 57, 163

Yoda (*Star Wars* character), 145

*I wish you much joyful weirdness in your life.*

—Gary Larsen

❁

# Carol Who?

Carol Weston is the author of several books, including *For Teens Only*, *Private and Personal*, *Girltalk*, and a series of novels about Melanie Martin, a New York City girl who keeps travel diaries. Now in its fourth edition, *Girltalk* has been in print for nearly twenty years and has been translated into Chinese, Czech, Russian, and many other languages. For the past decade, Carol has also been the "Dear Carol" advice columnist at *Girls' Life*.

Carol has been a guest on *Today*, *The View*, *48 Hours*, *Oprah Winfrey*, and *Montel Williams*, and has written articles, essays, and quizzes for *YM*, *Seventeen*, *Cosmopolitan*, *Parents*, *Glamour*, *Redbook*, and other publications.

A Yale Phi Beta Kappa graduate, Carol majored in French and Spanish comparative literature and has her M.A. in Spanish from Middlebury. She and her husband, Robert Ackerman, live in Manhattan with their two teen daughters, as well as a hamster named Buccaneer, a rabbit named Honey Bunny, and a cat named Mike.

Visit Carol online at **carolweston.com**

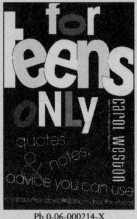

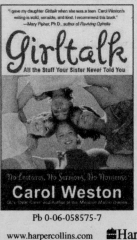